TABLE 31

BOOK TWO

G-L

THE ELEPHANT IS IN
THE SUITCASE

Prologue

Where do I start? was Anthea's first question. It's everyone's question at the beginning of a story. Every author's question from the first line of the novel is about to be penned. 'Is everything pointless? Those were the words repeating over and over inside her mind. If there is to be a beginning, a middle and an end, should I start from the end and work back?' The twenty-six characters all have one thing in common: a coffee table in a café, in Baker Street, London. Table 31, carefully chosen for many reasons, is a platform; it is the place of conversation amongst friends, forming numerous questions. Issues were constantly leading to old doors, chunky black iron keys and brick walls, gates, fences, and holes in the floor. Barriers that block the way through many frustrations ahead of the questioner. That is what life is about. A story based on true life experiences, about society's problems and who's right, who's wrong. About missing links to life's eternal questions. Many people call spiritual answers ridiculous or illogical. Something that cannot be proven always remained a mystery as if some information was missing.

Set across twenty-six chapters and twenty-six main characters, all searching for their truth.

A Life Well Lived

Anthea aged 99 years and 99 days. It takes 99 minutes for her life to flash before her eyes. She wrote her book before she turned 100, telling her life story and about how each person in her life has a story that affects her own journey. Life is complicated and relationships are convoluted in every living being, there are stories and messy family trees. In today's world, it is becoming more and more difficult to piece together a normal family tree. In fact, there is no normal. Each person creates their own normal, which is certainly very normal for this book. Let us say that Anthea's story is normal.

So, in a log cabin on the beautiful edges of *Lake Windermere*, England, her life rushes before her in a few seconds. Where do I start? Did the balls go completely mad inside the little brown suitcase and what really happened to CaféB? Did Poges and Anthea make it through to true love?

PROLOGUE

This story begins and ends with a Table.

But not just any Table.

A Table with an inner knowledge of the past, present, and future.

A Table with a soul that has come from the life force it was created.

Built and crafted from very special wood.

By Poges, the owner of the Café.

At the end of each chapter is a message from Table31 for all who read the book.

The next chapters will complete the life journey of Anthea

At CaféB Table31

ONE GIRL

ONE TABLE

TWENTY-SIX FRIENDS

THE TRUTH

IS IN THE

SUITCASE

G-L. BOOK TWO

Gerry [Uncle] Married to Yurgen

Gretel [Aiy's fiancé, Orson's sister]

Georgina

Granola [Indian married] Geraldine

Mr Grey [Sam Quentin] Gwyneth

Harriette Harali [The House]

Iris Ingrid

Jade Jan Jen Jeramiah Johan Josephine

Mrs Jones [School Teacher]

Katy, Ken [Producer]

Lavender Lily Lavinia Lucinda

G

CHAPTER 7

Grief

Geraldine-Gwyneth Georgina

Whilst looking at one of her old photo albums, at aged ninety-nine, looking back Anthea realized the more she grew older the more adept she became at enshrining the past. Her grandmother only had paintings and books to jog her memories and seemed rather contented. Nowadays, in the twenty-first century, year 2040, the world has an abundance of technological time preservatives. No need for albums and space cluttering photo frames. Anthea's mind darted back and forth between all her various decades of life. Writing her book on life was the most important thing for her with the few years she may have left.

Culling Blurry Photos

Remembering Geraldine and their times at CaféB was a wonderful experience to be transported back through time like a time machine.

1970. Photos, videos, sound recordings all at our fingertips ready to remind us and jog the memory of how things used to be. This makes moving on trickier, holding onto things make it possible to miss something potential today. Anthea decided to cull her photos over the weekend. Starting with the blurry ones, moving onto people she no longer liked or saw any more. Anything with people in them she tossed into the eternal memory bin and let eternity take care of them. 'Would this get rid of half of her balls' she wondered? Probably not. Grief lingers.

Most of the balls lingered like limpets on a rock. Many of them were like muscles and cockles. 'Difficult to open without a perfect tool,'

that thought brought her happy memories of summer Southend-on-Sea and Leigh on Sea. Two of the most popular seaside towns in England. All the happiness was there, the salty smells of fish shells, seaweed and pink, sticky rock.

Normandy Landings

Autumn rolled in sturdy and forceful like the waves on the Normandy beaches. Today was the anniversary of the Normandy landings during World War 2. Her mind was on her father, his part in the war and that thought led to the town of Angers, France, and the meaning of life. Oh, the grief that must have opened its mouth like a colossal unsympathetic sea monster and swallowed the families of those brave dead sailors.

Anthea saw Georgina and Geraldine fall in through the doors together acting their usual silly selves, laughing at goodness knows what. "Good grief you have arrived better late than never" said Anthea who was considering how much grief was in people's lives.

There was a book on the bookshelf called *Good Grief* which was not a subject Georgina understood however, she did appreciate the thought of robust company this morning with her three friends for two reasons. There had been family tension at the weekend and she was feeling a little nervous regarding her new job commencing in two days. "People who live in glasshouses should not throw stones.

They should take the logs out of their own eyes" said Georgina to Geraldine, Gwyneth's sister. "I don't think you have that right" interjected Anthea. "Well, the glasshouse was undoubtedly an issue in many families" agreed Geraldine "and I should know, take a look at my own family, it is destructive on many levels." Her edginess was made softer by her gratefulness.

Georgina had a mixture of both and delighted in the distractions at the café. 'People who live in glass houses was as confusing as good grief' Georgina thought as she sat around the table laughing and chatting, thinking, and planning with her best friends Anthea and Geraldine who were enjoying a much-needed bonding time together.

Georgina, finishing her hot chocolate, grinned at Poges on her way out knowing she had just scored a big contract for mini huts off the Orkney Islands, Scotland. 'Meeting with these clients this morning would not be anything like good grief or glass houses' she thought. She laughed and skipped out the door happily grief free.

Poges had the radio on as the last post was playing followed by the minute's silence. The gratitude, appreciation mixed with past sorrow, heartache and memories were evident on this anniversary. Some people lost their loved ones, their fiancés and never married. Anthea's Aunt Lily was one of them. Anthea was concerned about sorrow, wondering how much sorrow the many people around her had suffered in their lifetime. She felt for everything in life. 'We need bravery, getting up in the morning needed bravery' she thought.

Anthea's thoughts stretched the length and breadth of the English Channel to Christian and his father's cellar. Thoughts jump in leaps from one era to another so quickly. She needed to connect with the day ahead though it was filled with distractions.

Gwyneth, her Welsh friend was not born in Wales, nonetheless her roots came from there.

Poor Gwyneth was always at her wit's end and certainly at the end of her wit. She had no wittiness left. An amusing girl, light-hearted and loved making people laugh, had a quirky sense of fun. With curly bright red hair tumbling down her back she reminded Anthea of Lady Guinevere who rode a white horse.

Gwyneth was born in Banbury Cross. She had been suffering depression for decades, incompetently covering it over with humour. She had the usual extreme tiredness that snaps at the heels of hopelessness caused by the impending loss of three family members not necessarily by death. Geraldine had married quickly it was the death of her old life, all she loved and knew, good things that filled her heart for many years would be changed.

Granola.

She met and fell for a car salesman, an Indian man named Granola who swept her off her feet with charisma, gifts, and fun nights out in London. He chewed on the root of an Indian tree which became an irritating habit to all around him.

Something Geraldine could excuse as he was brilliant in every other way.

Granola loved movies and particularly loved Judy Garland who once said: "Always be a first-rate version of yourself and not a second-rate version of someone else." Geraldine felt special around him. He had an E-Type Jaguar, many friends and was as charming as could be. After all, the Savoy Hotel and Claridge's were so much more exciting than the local Brighton pub or a weekend away in Colchester. Geraldine needed to be adored due to the lack of love in her family as a child.

Their mother wanted a son which sadly for her never happened. She took her disappointment out on the girls. When Geraldine was eight her mother adopted a baby boy. She loved her son and they bonded as close as any mother and son could be. They slept in the same bed until he turned twelve. Geraldine felt emotionally orphaned. No wonder she was immensely happy at the thought of her new life with a car salesman who adored her. However, things were on the edge of change.

As her brother grew up, they all began to get closer. Her mother was looking forward to a nice son-in-law, and a larger family. However, a few months into Geraldine's marriage there was a quick change of plans and in a whirlwind the two newlyweds emigrated to India. Granola had given Geraldine no choice as to whether to stay in England or travel across the world to live in the hot, dry climate of Southern India. This involved change of environment, culture, climate, and friends. There she had no friends, no support system. She was bereft and dreadfully isolated as if half her soul was missing and with an emptiness that she could not replace.

Her husband had banned the use of a phone for the reason that she did not earn money for the bills. Social media or mobile phones were not yet invented and overseas calls were immensely expensive. He had so much control over her that she lost her voice, entirely unable to voice her opinions or requests to call her mother. The level of control was like a python winding its way around her neck, gradually strangling life from her. Bit by bit her personality changed and died. She was no longer the woman he married, that woman died long ago, she was a shadow of her former self, lost and unable to find the real self under the years of verbal rubble.

As their children grew over the years, they too learnt the skills of coercive control. It was like putting a frog in water and slowly turning up the heat. Eventually the frog does not realise it is dying a slow death.

Once a year she was allowed a monitored call to her mother or Anthea, but then again not both. What happened to her world? It was like a train wreck. A sudden uncontrollable grief hit her hard, she had lost everything. The childhood things she had collected over many years, her friends, her family all washed away from her life as if she had been in a sudden flood.

Coping Skills

She only coped by believing the time in India would be short, a maximum of two years. This was not to be. Her in-laws were unsupportive, cold hearted with little or no empathy as to her homesickness. Anthea quivered at the thought of the grief of everything to do with that situation.

The agony of the control exercised over her choices and life. Bullying concealed and abuse covered had been recognised in the media yet was still covert undercover.

Table31 shivered as if like a rumbling train had gone past. Anthea felt it; memories caused her body tremors. The ping-pong balls in the little brown suitcase winced. They echoed Anthea's recollections, ones she preferred to leave alone in the case.

Gwyneth had not yet arrived. Anthea was getting concerned and decided to work on her book as editing was like a glass of wine, it calmed her thoughts without making her tired. Opening her little book of quotations and inspirations flicking through until a quote she liked revealed itself and fitted her 'now' moment.

'I wanted to write down exactly as I felt but somehow the paper stayed empty' she thought. Yes, that fitted. Was the next page better?

She turned the page. Living in a house with no curtains, everyone could see what was inside. Her mother turned out the lights in a house with no curtains, but her fears had nowhere to hide.

She used to lay on her stomach and crawl under the windows so no-one could see her. It was scary for a five-year-old, her childhood home had no curtains because her mother hated them, because of the London war blackouts. Anthea on the other hand liked curtains to hide from the outside world.

The old farmhouse. Gwyneth often wanted to hide for dozens of reasons. The signs she read on a wall in a newsagent were most appropriate for her feelings that morning. Like Anthea, Gwyneth felt good when messages came from unexpected places and felt comfort, as if someone was looking after her.

CaféB was quiet for a rainy Thursday.

Sometimes the rain brought people in, nonetheless this morning it kept the hustle-bustle away which was a good thing as Gwyneth suffered from APD, Auditory Processing Disorder and could not think or speak when there was noise around her.

Her doctor suggested therapy which was both time consuming, expensive, emotional, and tiring. She was distressed at the distance, concerning her brother's new job, which took him and his family far away to Galveston, America where he had a challenging career high up in the world of Geoscience. It suited him well as he was a down to earth person.

However, their mother was beyond any comfort, distraught and mournful that her son and daughter had migrated so far away. A doctor came in to help calm her down, nothing helped not even medication, only a sedative by syringe lasting one day. All their expectations of a large cohesive family faded fast. Lack of time, busyness with work all meant the sisters never had time to grieve fully. It had a disastrous effect on the mental and physical health of both girls. It hurt knowing you tried doing your best and it still wasn't good enough.

Geraldine broke down and wept, Anthea passed her the white cotton serviette and patted her back gently, compassionately. Anthea indeed swallowed those words as if they belonged to herself and could not have said it any better. Geraldine continued speaking with scarcely a breath in between.

Geraldine's Letter

In-between sips of caramel latte she poured out everything she had written. Anthea could hardly catch a word.

"I wrote a letter to my father as it seems nearly impossible to communicate with him any other way. It is continually awkward, it upsets him, it upsets me and so it has come to this writing a letter. Everyone has had a stressful year in my family, which I seem to be responsible. I am not and I will never be held up for everyone's awful year especially my father," said Geraldine.

"Many things have happened in my relationships with family and things didn't work out the way I would have liked. People change, I've changed the way I think and feel. As you know Anthea, Gwyneth is not my true sister. We share a mother but have different fathers.

Common I know. I honestly love her though she's not my real sister" She went on explaining and sharing her pain erupting like Mt. Etna.

"It happened when we were eight and ten years old. I apologised for letting my father down and moving away from home all those years ago and went to live in Italy. Do my schooling. Then after a few years chose to live with my mother. It was an unfair choice on him I know, nonetheless for the best. I was continuously wishing to please other people but then never myself." Geraldine took a huge breath, gasping as she continued exploding her thoughts and words from her mind. "Now years later I choose only to please myself. When I moved out and found a friend to live with, I realised I had been in a tug of war. Three people in the war.

Myself, my mother, my father. It was hard for anyone to understand. It became hard to love my father due to lack of understanding. It was cruel. My mother interrogated me.

He questioned me and I became confused, I told him in the letter I was sad and sorry. I dreaded weekends and being told not to tell father this or mother that, I was in the tug of war. I felt like property between two jealous people. My mother got angry, each trying to get information out of me it was as if I had disappeared and only my eyes ears and body was there. My heart and mind had died, my mother remarried that's when Gwyneth came into my life. I had a different name to my siblings which made me feel odd. I decided to change it and that was the most overwhelming hurt for my father. It broke his heart and shattered his world apart. I could do nothing about it. Lots of my friends did the same thing and they survived.

I had to get used to step-siblings, learn to fit in and not be different. It was the worst torture for a child to lose sight of herself and have to remake a new identity. It was like I had died and came into a world I did not know. All the years seemed to roll into hours, time definition was hard to fathom. I was the only child and I wanted real sisters and real brothers not pretend ones. I constantly felt left out and not the same. I tried to explain to him and the expectations that he would understand were high yet unreachable. My father never understood.

People make decisions in life that affect and hurt others. It is inevitable and the pain never goes away. It is upsetting to the core of my soul. The emotional roller-coaster of choosing between two parents made me want to find me. The real me.

The one who now wanted to come together and stick both halves back together again. Like Humpty-Dumpty broken. I explained, I needed fixing and only I could do it. Step one was letting it all go and forgetting the whole past.

Nonetheless my father could not, so I had to break away from the see-saw. Swinging to and fro back in back out. It just couldn't work. I severed all ties with him. It was painful for us both.

He was my true father and I had to let him go. We lost contact for years. Father had a breakdown and I just had fun and grew up. I wanted to find happiness while he held onto the critical vision of my imperfections." Her lungs again refilled, she continued pouring out.

"We once made time for a coffee together, I went to the wrong café. I got the address wrong and he was so harsh on me. I tried; however, it was not good enough. Sometimes things just happen and they don't go right. Accept it! I yelled in my letter."

We both make mistakes yet somehow, I'm the one to blame. Of course, he is perfect. He has this air of needing to uphold a perfection façade which means I'm continually in the wrong when there's a problem. I've lost my sense of humour and I can't laugh at it anymore.

Glass Houses

Knowing he would hold it against me for the rest of my life and ask me for reasons. Why, why, why? That old blame game has become tiring and impossible to win. Yet I want peace. Peace in my brain, in my mind, in my soul. But as her father used to say, even a mistake may turn out to be the one thing necessary to a worthwhile achievement Everyone I have ever met is not up to your approval, not up to standard. I had met Granola of course; he was not good enough for me.

Nevertheless, I loved and adored him." Words kept pouring out. "You talk to me like I am a child, that's not what I want, I need to be a daughter and cherished as one."

Anthea Continued To Listen.

"I'm an adult. I make my own decisions I have tried to make you proud of me yet it never works. The bar is set too high, I will never attain it and so I have given up the competition. It is and always will remain the dog-shit on the footpath of life. I am just me. I have your genes and we can be friends or strangers. No blame, no-fault. Not a thing to be fixed. Just life I told him to let go and move on. I finished off by giving him my address. I had moved suburbs, a new county, a new postcode, new telephone number, new car, new home, new me. I still want a relationship with him Anthea. It breaks my heart to have to be up to scratch when he's not. Yes, he's brilliant and smart, but to me he's just my father." She lowered her head and paused.

"None of us is perfect. We all live in glass houses."

"Yes, we do" said Anthea quietly under her breath.

With a heavy heart she placed her hand on top of Geraldine's. Anthea's felt the balls in the mind rattle again. Many questions bombarded her. Gwyneth never arrived at CaféB. 'What happened to grief once dealt with, where did it go?' she thought. 'Where's Gwyneth, she might answer my thoughts.'

'How did a person work through grief when it was unbearable?' Anthea's thoughts unravelled like a badly knitted jumper caught on a barbed wire fence, she could not stop them.

Functioning during this time was doubly hard and everything took twice as long. The journey was traumatic harrowing and lonely. Journeys felt worse when everyone else was laughing and happy.

Grief and Loss

Anthea considered; grief came from being discarded. Left behind, like a puppy from a shop.

Bought and loved until it starts chewing up the groceries or chasing blackbirds and squirrels. Alternatively, the puppy that keeps digging up grandads' geraniums to hide the treasured bone then finds itself in a reeking pound. Unloved. It later became the preloved dog. Cute puppy gone.

Anthea decided to finish her chapter. She was writing her family tree into a book form.

Poges had made her an exquisite coffee and knew Anthea was writing the first of many books.

Collections of memories from Anthea's treasured meeting place of CaféB waited. She sat; pen poised. Inspiration oozed into her creative mind; Anthea was ready to begin. Her mind drifted back in time.

'Having had a sense of belonging, I enjoyed the fact I worked in busy London where my mother and father met. They met in an office, that much her mother had told her. My mother a secretary. My father an accountant at the London

Stock Exchange. My mother pretty and shy, my father was tall and handsome.' She respected and revered those memories, remaining close to those roots of her past and wrote 'Close to my embryonic, chance entrance into this world of survival and mystery.'

Anthea had done some research into her family tree as had Gwyneth. They both had a Welsh bloodline. Her father used to sing in the Welsh men's choir and had many memories of her father singing *Bread of Heaven* loud and grandiose from the shower each morning, probably thinking about the breakfast he was about to have mothers fabulous bread pudding.

Anthea continued to write until it became too noisy. It was a good thing Gwyneth had not turned up. It gave Anthea time to write and Geraldine time to pour out her heart.

Syndromes

A bus load of seniors came in, the café became shockingly loud with excitable people and it would not have suited Gwyneth who had several disorders causing her inability to think. Speaking and concentrating when there was noise around her was impossibly hard, due to her ADHD her ADD and her APD. 'These syndromes, disorders, and ailments we have to contend with these days,' thought Anthea 'Wondering how would it be in thirty years and in what manner the world would function?' Hoping not be around to see it.

The quiet morning rapidly echoed like a school playground. Seniors were everywhere.

Another excursion of a different kind. Bingo. Not an empty

table to be had. Table 31 seemed to have a unique vibration or radar around it, one that was like an insect repellent, repels all people or so it seems. Who knew why the table was continually free for her? That was one of the great mysteries. It was always available.

Mr Grey or 'could I borrow your salt man' was watching intently all the activity going on around his table. Who was this man that irritated Anthea by occupying a seat there each morning? She heard all his conversations and yet knew only that he was a crook and had a brother called Gerry. That was all Anthea could piece together, they had not grown up together but had met up in their adult life through a mutual friend called Victor, they were all at the same school together, yet Gerry and Mr Grey, or Sam Quentin had no idea they were brothers until they were fifty something. No wonder Mr Grey had a strange personality and did not trust people, had no friends as such and had twin personalities.

That morning, he was less than happy about the sudden invasion of people. People he did not feel comfortable around, seniors and the disabled would clear him out in seconds. To make matters worse, a car load of children all packed in like sardines arrived. They burst through the café doors.

Anthea enjoyed watching his face drop as he packed away his newspaper and pens, pulled up his socks and left quickly.

His table was snatched up by the large group of children all squeezing on four seats. He was never aware he sets those ping-pong balls off inside Anthea's mind. Awkwardly there he sat each morning. Not a smile. Once the children arrived it prompted his swift departure.

Anthea could not help noticing that he always wore bright yellow socks.

Anthea had a nickname for her little brown suitcase. Her annoying yet helpful little case and sometimes called it 'Valley,' Valley for valise. Valley, since you could not see over mountains when you were in a valley. A valley was usually covered in clouds. Valleys were your downtimes.

She craved the sunshine and the mountain top moments, not the valleys. Her subject to tackle this morning was relationships and family connections. That was not easy or quick and would take her a few years of digging deep into family history. The world seemed to be getting smaller and more people were realising they were related in some way.

We Are All Related

Anthea found out she was related to Poges somehow; however, they could never quite work it out. Life gets complicated. She was the daughter of his aunts second marriage. If there was one thing, they all had to learn it was to be accepting of each other's quirky ways, differences in opinions. The political discussions were robust, sometimes embracing their differences, sometimes not. CaféB had a good history.

It was once an old police station with a dozen cells then a medical surgery filled with many life stories, sick people, pain, and grief she imagined. Previously to that it was home to a museum, looking like a movie clip from the set of Downton Abbey, an ancient historic English stately home. 'One with a ghostly history, walls that held secrets, rooms that could talk,' Anthea continually thought, 'strange things like how many people had turned those brass door handles, what secrets would they have lived with behind those closed doors?'

She was feeling glad today, a far cry from the heartache and guilt of past weeks. Things felt lighter as if something was lifting, ping-pong balls were not allowed today. The girls were there so the balls could not come out to play. 'Do grief and guilt go together?' wondering whether grief compounds guilt and made it sadder, melancholier, and finding a way of disconnecting the energy of the balls. Guilt made pain more cumbersome, either way it was not a beautiful combination or recipe for peace. It was however, a recipe for depression, her thoughts on that subject continued like a machine gun.

Anthea found out her mother was born in the Salvation Army hospital. It was within the sounds of the 'Bow bells' which made her a true 'Cockney.' 'How exciting' thought Anthea when she found out. To her sense of adventure, it was like having a famous royal mother. London had a Knight, a King, and a Kingdom all in Knightsbridge.

Back at the sturdy legged Table 31, Anthea shivered, as if someone had walked on her grave. Anthea wanted to find out more regarding life as a 'Cockney' and her own birth. Where exactly did she pop out into the world take her first breath, shout her first scream? It was all a mystery yet to be revealed. Anthea found out the reason why Daphne had come into the theatre group, when Daphne finally shared her story with Anthea regarding their mothers, so comforting when a cause was discovered for anything in life.

The girls were planning a night out at the recently opened Mexican restaurant. Geraldine recalled how dreadful and humiliating it was when she was fired one night from her waitressing job. Many years back in her early days of marriage she had found a job at the local Mexican restaurant.

There she was all dressed in her black skirt and white shirt uniform….Embarrassment Geraldine felt sick and her overfilled sore breasts began leaking through her shirt. It was ok to laugh about it now, however it was dreadful at the time she was breastfeeding. Her night time job took her away from home and she missed her ten o'clock feeds. Embarrassed and wishing the floor would swallow her up having served up the various meals all with strange names she had not yet memorised. Looking insipid and the same colour, a burrito beige with a taco beige and white rice on the thirteen plates.

She delivered them all to the table. Placed them in front of whomever she saw needed a meal and proceeded to watch the patrons swapping the meals so everybody had what they ordered. Yet Geraldine's mind was on the baby as tears turned to sobs, the manager took her to one side handing her a small yellow envelope and told her not to come back.

Seeing all the guests at the large round table leave after they had built a mountain of rice and burrito with tacos on the top, humiliation took over as she jumped into her small green car and drove the fifteen minutes home. She had been sacked; it was a new experience.

She suffered post-natal depression; her husband did not cope well with that and her marriage failed shortly after the baby's first birthday. Geraldine became reclusive, rarely seeing family or friends. Anthea trembled at the memories that were shared at the table. 'How can life dissolve into such sadness for one person?' she thought. Therapy was not successful for Geraldine as she remained reclusive. She had a hobby farm where she raised a variety of small animals.

Catching sight of the new sign in the café garden brought a smile to her face, a smile with fondness attached. The unique hand-painted sign leaning crookedly against the tree read: *You harvest what you plant. A garden was a thing of beauty and a job forever.*

'I like that' Anthea thought 'garden therapy heals the soul.'

Golden Harvest

Georgina became the new sign writer for Poges café and was very talented having trained in Media Art and Carpentry. She thrived in her creative work. Her bubbly fun, wild hair and personality made her popular amongst the clientele and always had time for people and a cheerful word to make their day.

Motoring around London on her pushbike, she knew all the shortcuts and the little lanes. At weekends she caught a train to Wales, stayed four days, then back to London and was making a magnificent living building new *Chic Tiny Houses* in the Welsh town of Glamorgan.

Georgina loved it and would often arrange many a weekend away for the girls to all bunk down in a tiny house. Sleeping bags, laughing and munching on popcorn, jelly snakes and jelly green frogs were her favourites. Once a house had reached the lockup stage it was safe and fun, like camping but more comfortable. The girls would sneak inside and giggle about wild topics all night long.

Kissed a Frog

The café had a calm feeling, George Benson music playing in the background. Time was up; the girls departed. Anthea's thoughts were still with Gwyneth, you could hear them as if they had their own life which of course they did. Gwyneth needed to find her purpose in life, find her golden harvest. Struggling deep within her soul and not knowing how to reach it. She needed to be released from all the years of guilt and grief she carried from the broken relationships in her own mixed-up family. The great secret everyone wanted to know in life, needing a purpose to carry on.

Gwyneth needed to find it quickly. Anthea was worried and Poges looked sadly at her face, he too was heavily laden. Gwyneth felt as empty as her cup, something was up, there was a sense of not normal. It felt like a storm coming but nothing to do with the weather. Later that day Anthea received a phone call from Georgina. Gwyneth had been to see her mother. She had taken all her life savings out of the trust accounts having spent her life investing and had saved her whole life living on next to nothing. Hardly affording herself a coffee out. The biggest surprise of Gwyneth's life was about to come.

Gwyneth's mother had bought two round the world tickets on the Queen Mary Cruise liner for herself and Gwyneth. What a brilliant surprise. Gwyneth was quite overcome with gratitude that her mother had worked on a solution to improve her problem and was sincerely grateful and thrilled concerning her mother's new lease in life. They packed and left immediately with no time to say goodbye Gwyneth made one phone call to Georgina.

The cruise was a dream come true for them both. Gladys realised her purpose was to appreciate her life and release the children to their own lives. She felt a strong companionship with Gwyneth so it was perfect for them both.

The Grey Cormorant

They sailed the seven seas together for many years. Gladys lived to ninety-two, living out her days on the cruise liner stopping at several ports around the Americas, India, Australia, then New Zealand and every port in between.

One balmy morning as a grey Cormorant perched on the ship's railings, she passed away peacefully in her deckchair on the upper deck with her binoculars draped over her knees. Gladys had an ocean internment attended by the many friends she had met on board. Gwyneth had met and kissed her frog. The world of anguish seemed a million miles away since her ship wedding three months before Gladys passed into her next life.

Her mother's binoculars went everywhere with Gwyneth and her frog, feeling comfort knowing her eyes had seen many delightful sights through the clear lenses and had finally achieved clear vision on life. Depression sank to the bottom of the ocean.

Gwyneth missed her mother and was comforted by the memory she had reached a fulfilled life in the end. The grief of losing a special person seemed intolerable, unbearable, the cycle of birth and death, joy and grief is all part of life's journey. Her pilgrims journey. Often lonely. Like a suit, it's the only one that fits you.

Gwyneth missed the long talks with Gladys, they used to do

memory quizzes over lunch each day. Gladys seldom remembered what she had for breakfast yet could remember things like how in 1545 Henry the Eighth saw his flagship the *Mary Rose* sinking in the Solent north of the Isle of Wight. Gladys was a descendent of this family line and had a home passed down the family, with a lounge that had a huge central pole holding up the ceiling. The pole was wooden and came from the flagship. Preserved over many years, it is still to this day in the same house. The loss of an estimated 500 lives must have left many children fatherless and a great many widows. So much sadness in those days.

Today we deal with a whole world of different sorrows same suffering, different circumstances. The boat sank in roughly twelve metres of water. The wreck was discovered in 1971 and raised on the 11th of October 1982 in one of the most complex and expensive maritime salvage projects in history. The ships in Portsmouth had many a dark history and could tell some gruesome stories between the port and starboard decks.

Tiny Houses

Being inventive and entrepreneurial, Georgina had successfully developed her own company and had Grace as her business partner, designing and building *Tiny Houses* and specialising in treehouse designs. She was successful, enjoying the risk-taking, empire building, creating a much sought-after property development company.

Her houses remained small with people looking for different lifestyles. The treehouses were a roaring success making her a name in the industry, a growing reputation barely keeping up with the demand. Her designs were unique and individual, her marketing strategies were brilliant as were her songs. Georgina created songs in her television commercials that had the whole town and country whistling along to her jingles.

Often while playing the ukulele, she would sit outside the treehouses and sing. Some mornings she would break out into song around Table31, making up funny songs about certain people in the café. It was good for business, Poges loved it when Georgina made her surprise entrance, he always enjoyed a good laugh. Poges always said, "that girly has a mind that is so brilliant, that whatever she turns her hand at she would succeed to the top of her field."

CaféB was Anthea's Sanctuary, always her garden of Eden. The home of emotions lay as a memorial for all at the café who share their own experiences. Infinite aching stories for which one has a choice to live with or to let the suffering go into its rightful places in the history books. The family trees and the church records filled with sore, sad memories.

Anthea realised life was always a choice, to let go of grief. To hold emotion in your arms like a baby meant part of the loss remained with you. Life is a series of letting go. "Moving along" as her father used to say. "The moment has passed, the future's not here, the present is ours now. Be grateful for the good you find, the best of now and here." Being the poet that he was, he loved it when life and poetry came together.

Anthea had gratitude and appreciation for the sacrifices he made. Training the little brown suitcase to solve all life's questions and problems was proving an unsuccessful job so far for Anthea.

The balls were not organised, in fact yes, they have gone completely mad. She hid it well with trusted friends who were enormously helpful to her coping skills, helping keep anxiety at bay.

Lake Windermere

Many years had gone by since those precious days at CaféB and Anthea was now in the log cabin.

Writing was a necessity and a passion. She was aware time was running out. The London clock was still ticking. Though it no longer resided in her log cabin, the memories of it were still alive. The walls in the cabin and the trees around Lake Windermere still echoed from the days of the café though it was 290 miles from London. Wind still carried the memories. It is believed that memories have life and life must go somewhere.

Anthea heard the chimes and would tap her foot on the floor in time to the *tick, tick, tock* when she was deep in thought about the world today, now filled with insecurities, concrete housing blocks for the homeless and every spot where a statue once stood had stainless steel automated toilet blocks for the general public. Tokens were the new currency and a chip in the hand was obligatory. More privileges came if you had the chip. Refusal came with tokens at half the value.

Children turned against their parents and were rewarded if they did so. Governments with- held currency if the people rioted or spoke against the rules. Marshall law was the new normal.

History books were discouraged and often burned.

It was not an easy world to live in. There was protection over Anthea's log cabin though she never knew how that happened and couldn't quite work it out. That information remained off radar.

Lake Windermere was beautiful throughout the whole year and every season brough different beauties and pleasures with it. Most mornings a raven sang, more like a chortle than a song. Deep in the clumps of pine trees, she, or he, but Anthea suspected she for some reason, sang as if it were a message being given.

One morning, a bird looking like a stork carrying a baby, landed on her front porch leaving a cloth tied together with a package. Anthea opened it up to find a letter and a parcel of food. Signed, from Papa, in scrolled artistic writing.

Anthea wondered what had happened to old Papa.

He had not been seen for many years. Inside the package was bread, fruit, fish, and a box of wine.

Anthea was perplexed, nevertheless accepted things were strange and could not be explained. She read the note. The words spoke to her as if they were a voice. *"The day your life changed direction; was the day you wanted to please your father. That changed the course of history for your future."*

It took a while for those words to sink in, she always wanted to please her father, making choices that pleased him out of respect and fear, not herself. But it all backfired, she made wrong choices.

At night two eagles flew over her log cabin, every night. In the morning mist she was sure of having seen a shadow by the boat, with a cloak, it looked red in the morning sunrise but she was uncertain, as it was yet another one of those unexplainable mysterious things.

Anthea heard music and laughter brought in by the wind though there was little laughter in the world which was at war. Only this war was loss of freedom by stealth. Technology wars, country by country, thought police tracked and traced and exterminated any rebellion against the government.

People no longer got together but that was the protection given for the people, the care for the community and for the public good. Without a card, a chip or I.D you could do nothing.

Christmas, Easter, and any family tradition were long gone, lost to the lake of memories. The dead were cremated and turned into little acrylic blocks that the loved ones wore round their necks. Grave yards a thing of the past. Anthea knew her time was short. Her pen had to work day and night. With no electricity she relied on her lamp, which always seemed filled with oil. The more she used the lamp, the more it filled up. She had given up questioning these extra-ordinary things, nonetheless was grateful, gratitude was her strength. Contentment and peace were her clothing, understanding was her food, wisdom and knowledge brought by the raven in the form of little notes were her protection.

The ink dripped from her pen, there were others. Friends to share their stories, the pen poised, the paper awaited as she filled the awaiting blank spaces. Her delicate hand shook with anticipation of new words. The first word etched from the pen. Fruit.

Cafés all around the world have a Table 31, inspiring friendship, and conversation. A Table31 somewhere in the world belongs to you and always produces food for thought, good fruit to eat, and many crumbs of mysteries to follow, explore and find the truth within. …**This became her prologue.**

Anthea stared out from the window across the woods, watching the mist descending over Lake Windemere.

She saw the shadow with the red cloak once again. Yet there was not a house near the log cabin. The mystery begins. 'I know that cloak' she said quietly under her breath, leaving the condensation on the window.

The mist lifted, and the cloak vanished.

Anthea returned to her pen.

Thank you, Table 31, for wisdom and

knowledge to learn how to search for answers and the strength to carry it through.

H

CHAPTER 8

Humiliation

Harriette

Eighteen across. Eight letters, something in the room full of people. 'Well, that's easy' thought Anthea, Elephant. It has been following me around for years and I just can't shift it. At last, it has something to say, even if it is in a crossword.

This was a trigger for the balls to quiver and become annoyed. Anthea does not like problems she just cannot solve, so crosswords are a great therapy for her to ease into her day.

Harriette and Anthea had been friends over many years. They were used to each other's nuisances, immoral habits, and positive points. In this relationship, the good points out weighed the bad. Sometimes, worrying points can become beneficial, as long as there were not too many of them. It causes a deeper look at the issues.

Harriette was a notoriously late person, wherever she went, she would be ten minutes late, or sometimes an hour, usually because her diary was over filled with too many appointments in one day. She thought time would stretch itself to accommodate everything on her list.

To most people, this would be intolerable.

However, Anthea used the time wisely and sometimes even appreciated it. This morning,

Anthea had time to allow the calming thoughts to take their place. Hoping the mad balls did not erupt into a protest.

Anthea spent a few moments thinking about all the things she had in common with Harriette. Mainly, the sense of the absurd, thinking from left field and finding books with good covers. It feels good surrounded by likeminded people. However, there were times she did not enjoy community. This morning was one of them. Memories came to mind of a time where there was a work community project.

Everyone was asked to make something, representing their craft. Everything from cakes to paintings. Anthea remembered her clothing she made, beautiful hand painted tops that took a lot of time and talent to create the fashion items.

Harriette remembered her school did the same kind of fundraising; she produced 'shell jewellery.' Community markets usually produced a great atmosphere, connections time, fun, enthusiasm, and pleasure.

Anthea booked her spot and paid her donation money. Everything was set for the special night. A fashion show was planned and organised by a woman called Rosalinda and her models were all set to go. Anthea was thrilled to have been asked to participate. Community operating at its best. Music, lighting, all provided by talented volunteers. Anthea clearly had the best selection for the fashion show as it was her gift to put colours together.

Rosalinda had some clashing with Anthea and she was

insanely jealous, a jealous person by nature. Some people are just that no reason, just envious of every positive thing in people's lives. They thrive on the bad news, or the misfortunes and refuse to show happiness for the good times. Anthea was well aware of these personalities and she knew now as an adult how to deal with them. Give them *no air time* was her best philosophy and it seemed to work. 'Once you realise the problem, it is easier to cope with' thought Anthea. 'But it does not cure the hurt that some people are just plain horrid.'

Anthea would try harder than most to please everyone doing good things, she was generous, kind and had a warm, affectionate nature, sometimes to the point where she was exploited and undeservedly persecuted. Harriette and Anthea were the same personality and they understood one another. It was always comforting to have someone that suffers similar things and understands you.

The time came, Anthea and Rosalinda arrived at the same time. Awkwardly, the conversation between them was clumsy.

Rosalinda was ready for the setting up, organising and checking in. The large hall was split into areas and sections, Anthea's section was fashion, eight. Out of the blue, the organiser Rosalinda, ushered Anthea to a back room off the corridor, stating that the lateness of her application meant there was no room and therefore relegating her to a spot where nobody would see her garments and therefore did not get a spot in the fashion show.

No sales were made for her that night, her models sat stunned and redundant in the audience.

Community. 'Some people are just in it for themselves' thought heavy hearted Anthea.

Rosalinda was so jealous of Anthea's craft and skill, her ability to care and be kind to everyone in her path, that punishment and humiliation was delivered like a slap across the face. No preparation, just last-minute embarrassment, and dishonour. Adding to her anxieties, about communities. Shame swept over her body, feeling like crying and going home and wondering what would be worse. Staying for three hours or leaving via the only front door with all her stock. Either choice was like 'running the gauntlet.'

Poges was busy in the wine cellar, thankfully missing the full extent of her emotional downloading. She tried to find a way of fighting off her memories of embarrassment and humiliation. According to many people, some of the best times of your life were at school, before leaving for the big wide world, ensuing more boundaries. Now she was an adult and these things were still happening in her fully-grown world.

The time needed to gain knowledge regarding how best to deal with all the disturbances inside her head took years to attain. Anthea wondered if these situations had happened to any of her friends who meet here, frequently seated happily at CaféB.

The next half hour at CaféB centred on a family of five who were obviously on a day out with children. Their shaggy, beige haired non expressive dog sat by the courtyard window, unashamedly changing the energy and atmosphere in the café. The dog with the pink frilly bow in its hair became tangled in the chair legs. The four excitable children were playing a game which involved hitting, slapping, and grabbing each other's hands, laughing as each slap became more intensified. Two children knocked Anthea's chair several times, while their mothers, or carers were oblivious to the chaos this activity was causing.

Anthea glared at the parents. They were unaware their excitable little darlings were causing any havoc, unaware the child's dog had uncomfortably, awkwardly wedged itself between the children's feet, Anthea's chair, and a table leg.

She waited. She waited some more, wanting to see how long it took the distracted parents reading the latest *Dolly* magazine to wake up to the havoc they had brought in, to share with the entire café.

Anthea, with eyes wide open and looking like an owl was pondering on the self-centeredness of many of today's parents and children, how it was all about them, their needs and continual entertainment. Spoilt, fluffy dog was called *fluff*. 'How original,' she thought sarcastically watching the mother who now stood and allowed the sniffing to continue. Fluff wanted to sniff for as long as he took, Anthea observed knowing precisely what was about to happen. Yes, she was right on the mark.

On the way out, the little dog with the volumous pink fluffy head wear, cocked his leg, splashing the full contents of his bladder on the window by the chair, right where Mr Grey, was sitting. He grunted, shook his paper, glared at the woman who shook her head in wonderment and shrugged her shoulders as to why anyone would be offended at the dog's choice to do business wherever it wanted. Dogs had rights.

Anthea for the first time ever was delighted to engage in the vision of Mr Grey man snort and mumble under his breath. The family left, Poges sent someone from the kitchen to clean up the distasteful urine from the courtyards window ledge. "This is the modern family, dogs and children rule" Anthea heard a seventy-something woman say. "They are all the same in my opinion" she said to Myrtle, who was busily cramming her mouth full of a jam scone, wiping her face with a napkin in time to catch the sweet sticky goo rolling down her cheek and filling the deep scar she had on her chin. Myrtle had been caught up in a barbed wire fence, while driving a tractor across fields in her father's farm in a small country town called Ramsden-Heath.

She was a teenager at the time and recklessly assumed she was invincible. No fear about life, now at aged eighty-one she was however fearful of the modern society, the lack of care, or curtesy and terrified of crossing the busy London roads, in fact any road.

Harriette still had not appeared at the café, which left Anthea wondering if there was another train breakdown, as is often the case on hot days.

Anthea was getting a touch worried. If only walkie talkies or mobile phones had been invented, but alas they had not.

The Book Cupboard

Harriette and Anthea remained dependable friends for many years spending time walking through country lanes, finding wild flowers to press. The girls dried them, then turned them into framed pictures and ornamental lamps. The hobby was fun and lucrative. CaféB had a Harriette lamp in the female rest room. Back in the days of chivalry and manners, things did not often get stolen.

Today however, that would be snatched in an instant. Gone

are the days of chivalry and men holding a door open, or letting a woman in the door first, or a stranger helping with the shopping.

Cafés of all types were communities, where writers often met, the surroundings enhanced the satisfaction of writing. One thing Harriette had in common with Anthea was the fear of humiliation, both having been victims of embarrassment at school, for different reasons.

Harriette was caught in the book cupboard with a boy one lunchtime, hauled in front of the school assembly to be ridiculed and embarrassed. In those days that was normal for punishment.

Shaming and humiliation. These days, it is not allowed, as all have rights and there is no shame in anything. The word shame has left the dictionary. It has been removed along with many other words and definitions. Nothing is evil anymore. Everything is equal and allowable. Nothing is labelled immoral, that word has been deleted. Children have the most rights and are encouraged to use them at every opportunity.

Children as young as four and five are ready to exert their opinions and rights to eat dinner or have snacks before supper, or not hold a parent's hand. Life became complicated in the nineteen- eighties. Some rules relaxed, others were changed or wiped out.

Harriette's sister was married in Germany to her next-door neighbour Heidi, whose husband had left her for a Scottish lumberjack who was a champion in caber toss. There was only one family member at their wedding because nobody cared or had enough time to plan the trip to Germany. The shame reverberated through the family and their home town

Henley-on-Thames where some of Harriette's family resided.

Humiliation, shame, and disgrace took their place from that moment, bringing a lifetime of shame and recurring dreams. She still shudders at the memory of the assembly thirty years later, remembering traumatising things teachers did in school life back in the seventies. Hundreds of years earlier, it was even worse during Dickens time. Tom Browns School days and many other books like it demonstrated it well.

Harriette Arrives

At last, Harriette glided through the café door with a huge satisfied smile on her face, holding Anthea's favourite magazine, 'Harper's Bazaar.' "Look, I told you I'd find you a copy" she shrieked, placing the copy on the table. Anthea was thrilled that she was looking at an April 1939 copy that Harriette had sourced for her. Anthea was after a copy of the Virginia Woolf story *'Lappin and Lapinova'* and Harriette had sourced one from somewhere. She collected special magazines, ones with great articles of interest about Hollywood, or fashion week in Italy. This magazine was her prized find and Harriette was the right person to find it. Virginia Woolf books were stories Anthea loved ever since she could read, the books spoke to her internal world.

Anthea, having picked up a real estate magazine from the bus someone had left behind, sat back, savoured opening the pages, scanning the photos of beautiful homes. No mess, tidy kitchens, everything in order. 'Do not open those cupboards, check the garage or the garden shed' she thought. There the surprises lurk. Years of things you might one day use. All the things no- one else will ever want or need.

Harriette enjoyed talking about houses and they both loved the furniture. Small houses were becoming popular, it would become a growing industry. Certainly, in Georgina's world where boat-houses, barges, riverboats, alternative living styles were becoming sought after. Anthea was interested in the whole idea of a more modest lifestyle, less complex. More outdoor time, fewer electricity bills. However, that was her outside world.

The inner world was why table31 time was vitally important. 'Everyone should have one' thought Anthea. Back to the inside world where she was trying to understand her mind. The boundaries of her life were quite broken in places. Anthea sat with the comforting hot coffee cupped inside her freshly manicured hands.

They cared for one-another looking out for each other's well-being, understanding the complexities of their feelings. Discussing how humiliation can still cripple an adult many years after the event. It was an unpredictable bizarre journey, entirely stolen by another person at every stage of Harriette's life. She remained on guard, vigilant right into adulthood. Overcoming seemed impossible.

In the diary today was a planned boat trip for Harriette up the Thames River filming a documentary. A specialist in local waterways, travelling Britain as an environmentalist working for the government. She was a skilled, renowned scientist and had been nominated for two government 'Ecology' awards. The 'Kew International Medal,' sponsored by the Royal Botanic Gardens. Having produced and put together a massive project to film life on the river Thames, she was keen to share her work on the project with Anthea. Harriette had experienced some deep trauma at work by a jealous worker. It is always a hard job emotionally to recover from lies that are said about you over a long time, this is exactly what had been happening to Harriette. Yet she was unaware of the internal undermining of her self-confidence until she was accused of stealing plants from the botanic gardens at night.

Word got around the office that she had given herself an instant garden, which was quite untrue. Yet she had no resilience or ability to uncover the truth and defend herself. The person who was destroying her little by little from the inside, held a grudge. He wanted her job and she was better at the people skills required for the position.

Mentally she would never have coped but for her past experiences which helped grow her stamina and self-assurance. Harriette had triumphed over her years of being persecuted at school.

Something Harriette had said about "no time to rush to the toilet" caused Anthea to have a memory flashback. At school and subsequently at work, she would miss the cup of tea or the pee visit simply because of the inability to do both in that allotted time slot. Anthea had suffered with nerves at school each time she went to the toilet.

Sometimes the boys would peer over the top of the toilet doors, or under the doors, so most times she chose not to go. Peeing on the grass at the back where the trees grew was much easier. If she had to go, she allowed herself ten seconds to pee, finding that by counting slowly to ten, she could relax enough to do the job. Without counting, she could not.

This problem was first created at her childhood home *Harali* where there were too many bodies and only one toilet. Anthea's mother used to yell about taking too long and so the stress and tension built up over many years, until with huge relief to all, her father built a second toilet off the kitchen.

As a young adult at work, nervousness crept in, hand in hand with anxiety because Anthea needed time to pause, tidy up loose ends, making sure her skirt was not tucked in or bunched up and caught all puckered inside her undies. Rushing for time was the problem.

Fateful Day

It was on that fateful day in first grade, where her memories of school landed. The mere thought of it always sent her heart-pounding at the memory of children who sniggered and laughed innocently, she did not realise it was her that procured laughter, until her chilled flesh touched the wood of the chair sending goose bumps up through her spine. Sitting down on the cold hard school chair, only to find out her warm, comfortable skirt was missing. 'How could I have done that?' she thought, the cruelty of humiliation, a feeling she lived with, not knowing how to handle it.

Clamouring to find a way of fighting off embarrassment, lacking knowledge at that age.

Living with the feeling of being alone without the support of her loving family. No humiliation. No, not today. Embarrassment, shamed banned.

The girls chattered; their voices drifted out into the distance like a television with the sound wound down. Anthea's mind faded somewhere.

Where was Anthea now? Her ears ringing with embarrassment at the realisation the laughter was in fact at her. Crying deep inside, wanting to feel the comfort of her mother's arms.

The words in the beautiful old book her mother read to her each night without fail, the children's story of the little *Indian girl* who lived in a treehouse, finished with the line *safe in her mother's arms.* Anthea desperately trying to grasp comfort from words that were dancing like small fireflies, teasing, coming close. However, too hard to wrap her little fingers around. She often had a flashback of that old story. Secluded and cruel, with bully girls rarely caught or punished.

Teachers ignored the trouble in the toilets. It was frightening for her to go to the restrooms at lunch. She looked at the clock to see how long before it was home-time. Anthea, held on until home time, where bushes would accommodate.

When clocks were first invented, they had oscillating wheels and pendulums that swung.

'Loud dongs, long ticks that echoed in the halls. We have come a long way since' thought Anthea, however, no one has yet invented the mechanism we all want. Perhaps the ability to press the pause button, or the *speed things up button,* when we are impatient for those doors to open, for something to occur like the suitcase sorting itself out, or a back button, when we want to revisit a moment from the past, whether to appreciate it for a second time, or re-do it, make modifications, fix it, make it accurate, put things back together. A button for everything.

'Oh, so many things could be done differently' thought

Anthea. 'If only I had this piece of knowledge or piece of information, if only retrospect could help us all, we would live in a perfect world. With reviews, reconsiderations, we'd all sail through life brilliantly. Who does hold the secrets of time, who does hold time in his hands?' Pondered Anthea. 'Poges or Papa'? She wished someone did. Yes, this key had a purpose and once opened doors. Just as in life some doors close, new ones open. Doors which you may choose to go through, or you may be fearfully worried, nervous, choose not to. The balls shuddered at the risky thoughts, choices follow knowledge, understanding. Choices which were blind, deaf to knowledge and understanding, may likely fall prey to disaster. Such as marriage too quickly, or buying a home in a wrong street, or worse migrating to a country with opposite standards and cultures. Harriette shuddered to think of the number of disasters waiting for her, Anthea agreed they must avoid any traps at all costs.

Anthea's mother helped her to collect the floras on many walks with the younger siblings in the pram. Spending several hours walking the length of Goatsmore Lane where the cousins lived. The pushchair was constantly piled high with multitudes of colour, fragrances, insects that hid themselves inside the petals. Many had escaped into the woollen jumpers or other clothing by the time they had trooped home in exhaustion.

Heavenly Holidays

Mother's plans worked well. Exhausted before bed, she was always amazed they did not all suffer with hay fever. Anthea loved those happy memories. Her mother on the other hand did not have any happy memories, as sadness took up its permanent tent camping in her heart. She used to reiterate that living in a family means you're not alone yet so often it means you are. Sometimes even the best friendship can make you feel lonely when you don't connect in conversation.

However, some of the best times were had at school before leaving for the big world of time, travel, and more boundaries. Summer holidays, they seemed to go on for eternity. No pressure and such freedom, free choice, few boundaries. Now at table31, Harriette wanted to comfort the young Anthea, hug her with the protection of a mother's love. She said "there were too many children in her family and her mother could not cope with all the work." Anthea lived in the country and Harriette by the railway line in Romford. A busy town south east of London. Her father used to buy clothes from Romford Market and is still there today. Anthea particularly loved the red coat with the black fur hat, it was a coat she would have loved to have herself. That year, her father had visited the Romford market, He bought the coat for Anthea and wrapped it up for Christmas. Such happy memories of Christmas, snow, bells, trees, and traditional carols by real candlelight. The two friends enjoyed the fact they both had the same coat. 'It would be pleasant to live by a train line' thought Anthea, who lived in the dark shadows of a tree creaking country road opposite the supposed haunted grey brick farm house.

Anthea and Harriette used to meet up at *Harold Wood Park* in the school holidays. They liked visiting old grave yards and reading the names. They once got lost in Epping Forest, both their parents had to get the police to look for them.

Harriette was in trouble that night, she had been told not to visit the old grave yards as there were ghosts of past people who were unrested and graves that had not yet been filled in. What seemed a good idea in daylight, became an awful choice later on, the girls thought they saw a bride standing by the trees, in a white wedding gown. Perhaps it was her grandmother. They often used to see her and believed she was jilted at the altar. One night there was a man walking his dog home from the pub across the road, he had a Yorkshire accent, telling the girls the ghosts had things to deal with from past lives. Anthea said it was nonsense and Harriette remarked that only uneducated people believed in that stuff.

Cheekily, he said "If she did not deal with them, by moonlight, starlight, or fanny by gaslight she will be roaming these woods forever and a day."

The girls were not going to ask, or follow the strange man with the dog.

By six o clock the skies were black and a storm was coming. There were no warnings, no phones or internet to show maps or weather and neither of them could read a compass. Harriette always carried one in her pocket, yet never knew north from south. They were lost. "I wish I could read the stars and planets" she said to Anthea, "I'm sure we are walking round in circles" replied Anthea. It took a long time to recover from that night. Several weeks. The girls were not able to see each other as both had caught a bug that developed into infected lungs.

Anthea's aunt was often sick with lung infections from the smoky chimneys. She lived in Chigwell, on the edges of the Epping Forest which is mentioned in the Doomsday book of 1086. In 1253 Henry the third established the towns marketplace where the famous Epping sausage was created and sold in the thousands. The original church was established in 1177 and in 1277 Anthea's generational grandmother was married in that church.

Anthea and Harriette both loved histories, that's why they enjoyed graveyards. Filled with history. One of her best historical school memories was of first love. Everyone has a first love and Harriette could remember it like it was a week ago. The feeling of the heart fluttering, the butterflies in the stomach, the nervous shudders that oozed through her veins, she grew slowly in love with a boy from the grade above her and held hands all the way home from school.

However, her happy times were often short-lived by her insecurities, such as children laughing was constantly problematic, as she believed it was always directed at her. Now into her adulthood, it brought those memories flooding back, she wanted to remain unrevealed, hidden.

The invisible person she wanted to be was now somehow becoming exposed, just like a box with the lid taken off, she became exposed and needed all the relief she could get.

She needed to actively visit those awful old balls from the past. 'How much time was required to attend the inside of the petrifying case? Would it be disturbing? Inevitably it would bring sadness,' quite a scary thought and activity.

Anthea wanted a cleaned, cleared footpath through life. While still at the table she became anxious with bombarding memories firing at her whilst not allowing those ping-pong balls to take off. Dropping the bat like the boy did in the rounders game at school, she was for once, still in. The whole team laughed as her face became as red as a lobster in the middle of the high school field.

Anthea wished to be safe in her mother's arms, like the old story that her mother used to read each night. Mother was, after all her best friend. Humiliation hurt. There were times the ping-pong balls became agitated with extreme emotions. Often her emotions were out of control, exhausting, making her feel giddy, out of balance. 'Where do you go when there was nowhere to go?' she thought. 'Did emotions have boundaries when sharing them?'

Mystery Enemy

Later in the week, Anthea and Harriette enjoyed a bus trip to the theatre to hear the magnificent Hayden's piano concerto in D major. Her love of music started with her first concert inside the Royal Albert Hall, it was a family outing during those primary school years. Her mother and father used to take all their children to London, the place to go for concerts, live theatre, and movies. She was becoming well educated in the arts, the French horn and harp were her favourites. Played at the Royal Albert Hall, it was heavenly. This concerto brought the goose bumps out from hiding, so superb was the show, tears rolled down her cheeks like quavers off the music sheet.

The bus trip through London was all part of the wonder of the night out, Cromwell Road, where the natural history museum stands, a proudly magnificent building built in the 1870s, on the beautiful wide streets of South Kensington. Past the Albert memorial gothic structure in Kensington gardens, erected by Queen Victoria in memory of her husband Prince Albert.

If it were in today's times, it would have been destroyed by anarchists and protestors of history, no statue or gothic memory left. Anthea imagined Queen Victoria shudder in her grave. London today, with the unimportance of history, destruction was rife. Violence increased daily.

Endemic destruction of statues worldwide. "Thank goodness the dear lady is not here to witness it," said Anthea.

Porchester Terrace, close by, a street of large houses, Harriette shrieked out "that one for me" at a subtle price of six million pounds, or nearest offer 'and that was semi-detached' thought Anthea as the bus picked up speed, running down to Bayswater Road, through a few more suburbs, past Hatton Garden and Holborn Circus. The girls laughed about many silly things and funny memories together as they enjoyed the longest route possible to the Concert Hall. Well, it was after all part of the trip, finally arriving at the Elephant and Castle bus station, a short walk to the theatre.

High End Property

One of Harriette's favourite pubs was the Fox and Duck in Islington. It was her usual Friday night, relaxing with the live music, a relief to the stresses of her week. Rock-n-roll nights, Pink-Floyd nights, Electric light orchestra and Dr. Hook were her favourite groups.

Highgate is one of the most affluent of the London suburbs and protective of its conservation parks, gardens in abundance, it usually meant the pub attracted a more prosperous patronage, though not always honest with their dealings.

Undercover, covert crime amongst them was commonplace as was charm and wit. Harriette loved the area none-the-less and was always happy to get home from the noise and raucous laughter of the pub.

Parts of Hampstead Heath had three ancient kinds of wood and were all part of what was known as the Highgate Bowl. The village was mostly Georgian. Highgate boasted a large variety of shops, pubs, restaurants, and the old Victorian cemetery where the communist philosopher Karl Marx was buried. Some days Harriette liked to sit on a bus, time to chill, look out of the window from the top deck.

Catching a two six three or a one three four, she packed a sandwich and became anonymous. Her type of relaxation, alone, recharging time. Watching the beautiful architecture from the early sixteen hundred's pass her window in slow succession, along with the leafy liberal slow dance of Georgian homes. It was like a ballroom, the kind she loved.

Interesting place, Highgate, where the elite of global super-wealthy made architectural heritage their homes.

Harriette was a minimalist who found pleasure looking at the stately homes with all the furnishings, fittings, however, she vowed never to be a slave to one. Small was good for Harriette.

Sitting on the bus hurtling past the magnificent eleven-million-pound home 'Withanhurst House' a Queen Anne style mansion. 'Imagine the work involved in the upkeep' she thought, as she strained her neck like a rubber duck to get a better look. The next stop was Anthea's, she waved as the bus pulled away, leaving Harriette to enjoy the next few miles, indulging in her own thoughts.

Passing the second most significant private home after Buckingham Palace, three hundred million pounds, now 'there was a *home.'* Harriette loved to indulge her mind in this type of recreation however, a small flat of minimum simplicity was all she needed. She still loved and cherished taking these virtual trips into boulevards of the rich and famous, because she did not have to clean, polish or, shine those enormous windows, all the glassware, furniture, bedding. It gave her a great sense of pleasure. She loved the fantasy of high society, super-rich, top achieving professionals, all enjoying cosmopolitan lifestyles.

Academics to journalists, architects, pharmacists to surgeons.

Dusk set in as the bus turned into the last street, before reaching the final destination for the day. Her bus turned from Highgate into Southwood Avenue, into 'billionaires' row.

Notting Hill Mayfair. Jaw-dropping with stunning architecture and ornate gardens. Looking out of the bus window, Harriette recognised someone from the T.V Series, Monty Python. Her wide grin happy to be going back to her small neat, well-planned apartment.

Her father had banned anything to do with Monty Python from their home in her youth.

Many things were forbidden, it all seems a long time ago. Years go past quickly, we grow up, the clock ticks, socks get bigger, stockings get wider, changes never stop.

Harriette had to deal with the media department connected with her work. She enjoyed the meetings, the discussions about advertising, magazines tenaciously holding fast to their line of work, where no one edits the editor. However, she had to dodge the jealousy balls that hurtled towards her at times, threatening her existence within the job she loved.

Factual, honest reporting was critical, though not all times adhered to, poetic license to exaggerate sometimes slipped in. The high gloss, photographic magazine called 'London's Endeavor' on the environmental conservation of London, Great Britain, meant Harriette was right up with many clear-thinking people. Intelligent minded editors, politicians of every calibre, her thoughts were on both sides of the coin, she could blend with combinations of all sorts of people.

Why should feelings of humiliation caused by jealousy stop her from functioning? Some days she doubted herself, other days confidence was her friend.

Hold the Test of Time

Those old homes had stood the test of time and were still standing. So, could she. No covert enemy was going to squeeze her out using humiliation as a weapon, creating nervous energy that would someday eat into the blood vessels. 'If the enemy didn't kill me, the clot would,' she thought. The well-built, good quality, self-assured, individual, stunning architecture; barring an earthquake, or a war, would be standing long after she took her last breath. Thus, her inspiration to keep going came from buildings of stature.

Anthea vowed to stand by Harriette in her darkest places, allowing no insidious gossip caused by jealousy and envious colleagues to come between them. There was one thing the table had taught them both, hang on for the ride, it might be rough. Stand firm, become like a big building built on a rock, withstanding the storms of life. Hold onto what is right and fasten life's seatbelts. Appreciate the ride, the simplicity it brought her like a gift.

Harriette arrived home. Put her feet up, threw a blanket over herself. A glass in her hand, a Coffee Martini. A nourishing bowl of smashed Avocado, refried beans. She put on a DVD and indulged herself in her favourite movie.

Notting Hill A Favourite Movie

A few minutes before the movie began, Harriette made a phone call to Anthea, having just seen an article in the 'Homes and Gardens' magazine on tombs and graveyards throughout London.

Hampstead heath was part of the bus trip they had just finished and was mentioned in the article. Thinking Anthea would still be up, she called and shared the historical fact that John Constable was buried in the family tomb in Hampstead London, along with his children. The phone call lasted another hour. Hugh Grant was forced to wait. Anthea was thrilled with the extension of their conversations, it left her needing the next clue, knowing it would come somehow from the new painting Poges hung in the café that morning. Tomorrow Anthea with look at it and get her message. They always come.

Hampstead Heath.

Who did she know came from Hampstead Heath, with significance to her life? The morning would reveal her next step. Poges had a new sign in the garden.

"A healthy attitude is contagious. Just don't wait to catch it from others. Be a carrier."

[Tom Stoppard].

Thank you, Table 31, never weak, never fragile. Healing, giving a home to the past secrets yet to be revealed.

I

CHAPTER 9

Iris Insecurities

The Ibis Bird

If someone throws a stone at you, throw a flower at them, remember to throw the flower pot with it [Minions].

Iris was bullied her whole life to the point of losing faith in her ability to decide. She would feel sick and vomit if she had to make a choice. Fear gripped the back of her throat, rendering her unable to speak. Fighting back, frustration at not being heard were the two things that followed Iris all the days of her life. Insecurity will always lead to people pleasing and that is exactly what Iris did. She failed because it led to everyone controlling her. Iris lost her sense of worth as a person, as a human and therefore lost her identity.

Whilst her intuition was sharp, she belittled it by calling it a hunch. "Oh, it's just a hunch" she would say, when in fact her hunches contained some of her highest and most profound insights and wisdom. Iris needed to learn to take this very seriously into her decision making. "Don't get to the point where you need to throw the flower pot" Anthea told her one morning at the café.

Anthea had been to the market during the week and found a flowerpot to give Iris to remind her of this conversation.

Poges had been to the Notting Hill market and found this old sign at the bottom of the pile of other people's junk, about a stone being thrown at you. He found it amusing and was a collector of strange sayings and other things. After polishing it with linseed oil and elbow grease, it became the new sign in the garden at CaféB. The saying was about time, *there is nothing new under the sun.* Time did not matter to her; it was a way of measuring the seasons. Her mind wandered into profound places; memories of past relationships dominated her thoughts.

Today Anthea was seeing Iris, always a lovely meetup and they always went longer than planned. They laughed at deep things, cried tears of hilarity, it was always great therapy. Talking about 'Poges' Art was always good therapy' thought Anthea.

One painting, a favourite of Iris, was an Ibis bird eating the wheelie bin lid, set on the Gold Coast, Queensland, Australia. Another, a painting of an old letterbox from a famous London Street, Kensington. Yet another piece of art was of a Magpie attacking a bicycle helmet in Melbourne painted by a member of the drama group from Australia. Apparently, *Magpies* were a real problem in Melbourne, they were disliked,

especially around the AFL footy season. Well, they were a pest anytime, Anthea heard. The Ibis looked as if it belonged to the Jurassic era. Having a long scraggy neck, a long black snappy curled beak. Looking like a pair of hair curling irons.

Coffee arrived. Iris was late, people always seemed to be late. Anthea did her usual newspaper word puzzle while she waited. From hibiscus, she made the word Ibis. Totally engaged in her word search from a crumpled old book stuffed inside her bag, pencil stuck inside the furrows so as not to lose it. She had always enjoyed a love for words which were like 'flowers to a bee' colourful, tasty, fragrant, attractively written when presented on a blank white page. She could find words, yet she was unable to find the meaning to her self-doubt, lack of confidence, or reasons for her uncertainties about life. 'So many people in the world, never know why a friend turns on them,' thought Anthea. 'It always causes distress and insecurities' wondering why Iris was late.

Self-Inflicted Pain

The café door flew open, Iris raced in, sat down beside her. Face flushed, she burst into tears, spinning her words out in a jumbled tangled fashion. All tousled, like matted hair.

Multicoloured, full of different subjects all in one sentence. It had all the beginnings of a tough morning ahead.

Iris took in a large gulp of air, shook the curls from her shoulders as she took her seat at the table, removed her coat, and wasted no time releasing her thoughts and made way for the conversation to flow with Anthea. A gusty wind blew open the café doors, March had arrived, the unpleasant cold nights finally ended as March rubbed shoulders with February. with a vengeance, raising every hair on bare necks in CaféB.

Iris had fallen out with her sister over differences of political opinions. Anthea could still feel the memory of the many people who shared a part of her life for years. Some now gone for various reasons, most had remained good friends.

Around the age of two, Anthea's sister was born and became a significant player in her world. Iris seemed to share the same scenario.

Both their sisters now in their sixties, had withdrawn from family and gone their separate ways. Iris, had no relationship with hers.

Having felt sad for many years, after fifteen years of trying to fix and mend, decided life was uncomplicated and clearer without her sister. Clear, like a clearing in the forest, where dead trees had been felled to make way for new growth. Clear enough for her mind thoughts and feelings to fly free like the Ibis bird, eating anything and everything without judgment, or shame. Iris was fascinated by the Australian Ibis bird.

A relationship included three main ingredients for Anthea, a bond, an alliance, an acquaintance. All three were valid. All three were both necessary and essential for a relationship to work and just like electricity, there needs to be a connection. Iris loved the bond between friends the best. A partnership was essential to her for building trust. She had lost the relationship with her sister through various family breakdowns. Her sister was irritated by the many issues she held in her head. She either hid it, or showed it. Both were uncomfortable to be around and it affected their bond, brought insecurities, doubt and mistrust between them.

'Anger only ever hurt the angry person' Anthea remembered reading once and tried to recall the statement to Iris who had to deal with her own various levels of annoyance and irritation which stemmed from anger about being stuck where she did not want to be.

Always wanting to please other people and her family, her sister, her father, so her life choices were made accordingly. Now she was stuck in a life she did not want. Unable to explain herself she stared out of the window. It was as if the windows were crying, the beads of condensation dripped from the glass panes on that cold, wet morning, mainly because of the steam from the hot coffee machines whipping up the many varieties of queued coffees, yet, if windows had insight into our lives, you'd call it empathy, not condensation.

Iris had a headache, blamed it on the Martini from the night before. 'It had nothing to do with Martini' thought Anthea, even though she had made it in a large Indigo coloured glass, the size of a mug and sloshed the Martini, rather generously.

Self-inflicted pain was rarely going to get any sympathy. Iris remembered her mother shouting to her once "self-inflicted" when she and her sister crashed noisily home drunk from a raunchy wild basketball party one Friday night and threw up in the laundry sink. Well, it was probably early Saturday morning, filled with fear of being caught out by their father, coming home later than midnight.

Memories of the creaky floorboard as she climbed the staircase always made her shudder.

The feelings of guilt still raw in her mind. Those were scary times growing up. Now, years past, Iris has no-one to share memories they could laugh at, no-one except Anthea. Iris, not having a good day, sobbed into her coffee, at the waste of many years.

Such waste. "Where do those years go?" she asked Anthea. "I wish there was a holding bay, where you could climb back in and change a few things"

"A typical human thought" said Anthea, wiping away a single tear from Iris's cheek.

Iris Never Lied

Iris talked for a couple of hours. Her first sentence was that some people were helpful, though not liked. She had a friend at work. Many of her work places over the years were full of this type of friend. Anthea also remembered feeling insecure in one friendship and became so anxious she sometimes vomited at home after work.

She read in a book once that the definition of a friend was *a person who loved at all times*.

Someone who sticks by you through thick and thin. In the droughts, the harvests, storms, and sunshine. Friends and family, maybe without them there would be no pain. Iris relayed the story of her very close school friend, telling Anthea that she had that friend until her marriage crumbled. Iris told her school friend, her neighbour, her sister-in law, and it was as if everyone scattered like mice when the lights go on. She hardly ever saw that old school friend again, even her mother distanced herself which manifested in a type of condemnation towards Iris who felt her entire support network had disappear.

Another trusted friend offered Iris shelter from her intolerable situation. Her mother disapproved which made the relationship with her eternally awkward. Some days, Iris, who never lied, hated lies, found herself lying to save her relationship with her mother. She was so distraught and dispensed her grief out onto the table. Her biggest fear was

'Loss.' This impossible situation seemed un-fixable leaving Iris locked inside isolation and insecurities. The café was noisy and offered a safe place for the flow of tears and tension to fall into the wood grain of table-31.

Iris loses Friends

Throughout this time, Iris spoke out, she became vocal, she learnt to unashamedly express all her feelings, holding nothing back to the point of offending with her truth. The pendulum had swung, she became more isolated. Did it matter?

Feeling rejected by her mother and her old school friend; she was not sure of her future. This was a frightening situation to be in.

Iris relayed more information to Anthea about her mother, who took care of her brother, bought him a car, gave him a home to live in and supported him when his marriage failed. This made the relationship worse for Iris between mother and brother. Mother was not fair or even seemed to care about Iris. A marriage breakdown brought shame into the family, yet there were three members of her mothers' family who had successfully re-married, were happy and it had not affected the wider family.

Once loving, kind and thoughtful, Iris had changed. Being kind and a good friend served her no favours, she became the opposite. Opiniated without boundaries, friends could not handle the new vocal Iris. Friends are trees that bend and break, they eventually snap. 'Did everyone have these people in their lives?' wondered Anthea. 'Ones who were either the discarded or the discarder, where the abandoned were left wondering what had happened' The insecurities, the mental turmoil inflict considerable damage where there was no safety, no trust. 'There was a compartment of the brain that felt insecure at all times' thought Anthea. Insecurity was a terrible feeling as was injustice.

When out on a work bonding night several months previously, Iris tried to be sociable. For some unknown reason a particular co-worker Hilda, ignored her completely. There was going to be no bonding happening that night. All bets were off regarding any reconciliation. "What was the point of work bonding nights?" said Anthea, Iris simply threw her head back and carried on with the description of this night when a friend Helen had asked her for money to help with a speeding fine.

A week later, another bonding night, the same friend Helen, asked Iris for money to put towards a holiday she badly needed, yet could not find the deposit for the accommodation. Iris had always been the people pleaser and was used up by pleasing everyone.

The bonding night was a trip to the orchestra in the city. The atmosphere was sticky, tricky, sickly like a dripping cake, where the icing had all fallen off on the floor. What should have been lovely, was now onto the floor. Irretrievable.

Iris never found out, what this co-worker's problem was towards her. Not knowing the issues was worse torture, causing covert mental abuse. Iris suffered mental disturbance that the idea a bonding night works, this failed. The whole night left Iris hurt and confused. 'Whether it was Hilda or Helen, or her mother Ingrid, why did Iris allow this to go on?' wondered Anthea who had known Iris for several years.

Iris articulated her pain about the way her children misrepresented her. Her husband made her feel worse by accentuating the fact maybe Iris was insane. "Insanity" he said, "runs in the mother's side of the family so it was plausible" according to him and needed to be considered.

'Iris's well of tears must be running dry by now' thought Anthea, as she handed her a wad of blue serviettes for the waterfall. Iris continued to unravel her distressed mind squeezing crumpled tear-soaked paper and continued to describe the pain of being misunderstood by those dear to her simply because she had different opinions, politically, emotionally, socially, unable to defend herself amid torrents of emotional abuse. Lies, disregarded respect tear flesh from the bones of your life. It seemed as if all the insults tearing at her flesh were done for the pure amusement and gluttonous pleasure of those around her.

During this period, which went on for numerous years, Iris tried to tolerate it, make it better. She was kind, pretended it was not happening, shrugged it off. If she made any hint of a complaint, it would be self-inflicted to her detriment.

Iris was accused of being over reactive, over thinking the situation, over sensitive and could not take a joke. It was as if the family member or close friend who delivered the blows, fed like hungry vultures on the flesh, feasting on the sadness and emotional pain Iris now caried.

This pain was unbearable and unjust, there was no reason why Iris should be so dishonoured. It was a nightmare she could not wake up from and she needed a representative who would stand up for her honour, an advocate but there was none. She had no one in her family who would stand strong for her, they were all frightened that if they did, they would become the next victim. The kinder Iris was, the worse and uglier the situation became, "perhaps kindness feeds the angry bull" she said as she grabbed more serviettes.

Invisible Shame

Iris expressed suicidal feelings and believed the only solution from the pain of betrayal going on around her was the exit door. Symptoms of depression, despair and hopelessness were fast unveiling themselves, her heart was sick, her hope for a new life delayed. Iris knew she was not mad, far from it. Neither was she insane. Some people would disagree with her and say that "anyone who contemplates suicide is insane."

The problem tried to reveal itself like a salmon leaping upstream, landing 'slop' right before her shocked eyes. Anthea was deeply worried about Iris; electric currents ran through her flesh at a hundred miles an hour trailing intense anxiety with it. Her whole body shuddered, quaked at the thought. The committee inside the suitcase were unable to do anything at this point. The *insignificance balls* jumped right through the rings of fire, the gnashing teeth of the boundary monster. *Weak, insipid balls* had tough armour on, they were the bullies and were out of control, thumbing their noses at the compartments, the little brown suitcase showing the strength they had to ruin any moment during her day. There were times she could control them and times she could not. This was that time. So, Anthea took a deep breath, determined to roll with the punches.

Boundaries were necessary to make the world go around

perfectly, they had a designated job to do in her outside world and determine the compartments in her inner world, determine the size, dimensions, how large or small each compartment had to be. Thinking and trying to find answers left her tired, the *black dog* always snapping at her heels was tiring. No wonder depressed people sleep a lot, it was exhausting sorting boundaries. Oh yes, the little brown suitcase, had a lot to answer for and those answers had better start revealing themselves. She squirmed on the seat, feeling awkward and uncomfortable somewhere inside.

"Dreadful Ingrid" Iris finally spat out her name. Her own mother was feeding from the pain Iris displayed. A mother who relieved her own issues by being cruel to her only daughter, openly favouring her son. Anthea mentioned that it was a game some people play, a power game, wrapped in envy, jealously coveting what Iris had, yet she had nothing of any true earthly value. Iris forgot she was in the café and wept. Poges brought them both an *on the house Irish coffee*. "Always good to have before work" he said with a grimace on his face.

Iris had dried her streaming eyes and finished the story ready for her response and was aware her story echoed Anthea's past family memories. How did one unravel the web of complicated personalities to find where the truth was? This kind of character slaying, onslaught by any person or persons, family or close friend had left her mind spinning. Portraying the spider spinning the perfect web to catch the prey and Iris knew she was the inevitable flesh destined to be destroyed. Iris began to wonder if two people could lead the same life, mirror each other's situations. Things appeared uncannily similar.

Bonding nights came up all too frequently for Iris's liking, as she found them exhausting and would rather not participate. 'Sometimes you do things to please others and to look popular' thought Iris. Why do we do that? She wondered, but she did not have the self-confidence to say no to anything.

There was another work bonding night coming up, Iris was dreading it she simply could not fix this problem, because there were people in the office who made life miserable for her therefore decided it was time to leave the job.

Once again, decisions based on other people, changed her future. For better, for worse, she was to find out. A magazine on birds perched on the table edge. It was not there when they arrived, maybe Poges put it there, it did not fly there by itself, nor did Anthea bring it with her. Iris made a comment regarding the Australian Ibis bird, which intrigued Anthea. No one liked the Ibis birds. Iris saw something of a message for her, Ibis birds were never appreciated yet were not insecure either.

Iris wanted to be the Ibis bird, be herself, not worry about insecurities, not wanting to be discarded like the rubbish in the bin, she wanted to be suited to her job too and was feeling unsettled, with inner turmoil. Anthea could do little to help.

Worry and insecurity instead sat securely on her shoulders. 'What did this unpleasant colleague have against me, did I do something she didn't like, have I offended her, is she jealous of me for some reason, just because I wear a size 10 dress and she is in a size thirty, my bank account is swelling and hers looks like a flat tyre, I'm popular and she is not, I have a husband and she doesn't, what is it?' thought Iris who needed to find the truth, yet could not.

Insecurities

'How did truth and a kind heart help Iris?' thought Anthea, whose isolation balls were jumping boundaries with her insecurity balls. They had been settled for months, now needed reassurance. Anthea needed more relaxation before tackling the worm, which was her name for the London underground system. 'The giant worm of the underworld. There were plenty of boundaries here' she thought. The worm in the outside world had a management department and without it nothing runs smoothly and everything grinds to a halt. Was this helpful thinking? Everyone deserved the right to be appreciated, valued, cherished, respected, and loved.

One thing regarding table31 was that it contained every wild conversation expressed over dozens of years. Every word soaked into the wood grain, spills nothing. Anthea contemplated the idea of hundreds even thousands of conversations making up the flesh of the table. 'Where did they go, what happens to the energy of all the words, hopes, feelings, thoughts? Do they die when a person dies, or are they part of the table grain forever?' she wondered.

That evening, Iris arrived early to her Indian restaurant job. She was determined to turn a new leaf, put it all behind her and be the best worker, the best friend that anyone could be. She had a smile and put on a spring in her step, served meals with a cheerful happy tone to her voice.

Energetically mopped the floors, cleaned the kitchen until it shined, it felt like her back was going to fall apart.

Iris was called into the main central office later that night.

She tripped over some rubbish left behind by the messy birds, usually crows as she stumbled through the side door, smiling and humming she had waved goodbye to the last worker. Heart racing, she took hold of the envelope handed to her. Mr Ingleton, the manager, handed her the envelope with a half-smile and two weeks' pay in it, a formal letter with work related information. He thanked Iris, telling her she would be more suited in a different job and told her they were letting her go.

The inevitable happened, insecurities flooded in as she left the office, she felt her stomach heave, as her throat swallowed the confidence she had been developing with Anthea's help, having once reminded Iris of a statement about clowns and makeup on a billboard advertising the next play called *Circus* all about people trusting true friends and finding out they wear a mask.

The actors with their makeup on portrayed your friends, but then again when their faces were cleaned, who was looking at you then? What would Iris do, aged fifty-two, how would she survive into her old age? Anthea would always be there if she could. Iris knew she had to either live by herself on a rural property, breeding dogs or goats, or her second choice would be to do what her aunt did. She contemplated putting her head in the oven of her London flat, but instead booked onto a round the world lifetime cruise, cashing in her savings and travelled for the rest of her days.

Now Iris had to decide, something she had no ability or faith in herself to do. In the distance she heard music playing and the sweet voice of the singer…. Tagore.

"I have spent my days stringing and unstringing my

instrument, while the song I came to sing remains unsung." [Tagore] Iris bent over a patch of bluebells in the grass and vomited.

Thankyou Table 31 for the truth of good faithful friends, for comfort in times of distress. It surely is the truth that sets you free.

IT IS
ALWAYS

THE
ELEPHANT

IN THE ROOM

J

CHAPTER 10

JUSTICE

Josephine and Juniper

Judgement is not a pleasant journey and jealousy worse. If anything in this world eats you alive, keeps you as a prisoner, spits you out with no dignity, honour, or respect, it is these two greatest of the soul's enemies, like a trainer in a lion cage, you can't always tame the animal, sometimes it devours you first. Anthea had strong emotions all her life which was 'an obstacle,' she thought as she stepped in a pile of rubbish that had blown up against the café doors in the wind. The gust of wind came from nowhere, it was dustbin day.

There was the usual rubbish blowing around the un-swept, dusty streets on a Friday. Fridays were also good introspection days for Anthea as she watched her life go by like a movie, looking at things from every angle, putting herself under the microscope to see where the pests are.

Red Bus Clock

The enormous 'Red' clock on the wall of CaféB was in the shape of a London bus. The time keeper kept the café in order. It tells Anthea the time to leave her comfort place each morning, so she could be at her place of work at the correct minute and second. Harrods, Knightsbridge London where she ran the evening dress department on level one. You were not allowed to be late; it was frowned upon.

London, notoriously famous for history was an exciting place to write. Sitting at a café was possibly the exact opposite of sitting at her window at home. Here she saw smiles, briefly engaged with people she knew. It was an engagement of the eyes followed by the heart,

which created a soul connection, bringing a happy smile. A joyful thing, a warm human thing people did when there were no earphones involved.

These days in 2040 are different. Screens the new smile. Everyone smiles at their *screens*, it was a strange new world for Anthea now, engaging with a screen was not nearly as much fun. The one good improvement is each time you smile, the phone takes a picture of your teeth and show all the potential cavities. In Red. Cavities that are ignored show up as green. Every photo will show red or green until the problem is fixed. This invention in technology has cut down the number of selfies. Very few on public transport take selfies.

People pulling faces, unaware, with no care, others watch and make mental judgments, never in the open, just in the thoughts. Judgments about everyone and everything. Selfies are as it says. Self. The new order of the day. 'Mobile screens of the now present period, were purposefully employed to prevent any source of outside interaction' thought Anthea.

Young mothers, any mothers, all pushing prams with babies through to toddlers, looking at screens. Mothers with white tipped ears, talking into the air. Conversations loud and out in the open for all to hear, oblivious to the natural interaction of a small child in a pusher. Few books, screens the new babysitter.

Anthea sat in her usual spot at CaféB, gazing out of the pretty window into the busy, bustling street, ankle deep in snow, with Christmas decorations hanging from the lampposts in readiness for the season of great cheer and expensive carparks. Giving and receiving, happiness, love, and good cheer.

Rubbish bins overflowing with empty bottles and cardboard packaging.

She took in a sharp breath; something was amiss, feeling anxious as she opened her post, she had received a postcard from Jade who had been on holiday and had visited her family in South Africa with her young daughter Jarrah. They would be away for three months; this was month number one. Jade enjoyed working in the Harrods shoe department and loving her job, it was safe, clean, sociable, and girly. Anthea was already missing her.

Jade was born in England, in the most beautiful county of the Cotswolds. She migrated as a small child to South Africa, in the area *Benoni Transvaal* with her parents at aged three. Her father worked long hours in a factory making car parts for Jaguar. Her mother was a dental nurse. Jade was brought up mainly by her black nanny, she was sometimes taken to work by her mother, when the employed nanny was sick. Life was different and Jade learnt that segregation of colour was normal, with different shop entrances, different beaches according to your colour skin and the two never mixed. Blacks separated from whites and coloureds was a normal way of life. If you were white skinned you lived behind locked gates, high walls, and bars at the windows of every house.

Jade came back to London when she was twenty-six, it was a shock to her nerves. Everyone mixing in public was a threat to her safety. Public transport was crowded with people of every colour. Shops had one entrance, which everyone used.

Jade had been diagnosed medically with *Post Traumatic Stress Disorder*, meaning she was continually living on the edge of nervousness, jumping from her skin at every loud noise and she had a permanently elevated heart rate and had suspicions that a hijack was imminent. Therefore, she was constantly in a *fight or flight state*. She could not cope with driving a car in case she was hijacked at the traffic lights which had been a past experience in Johannesburg.

Once Jade was employed at Harrods department store in Knightsbridge, she and Anthea became friends. They met in the cosmetics department, buying lipsticks during one staff lunchtime. Their friendship grew over years, because of the experiences Jade had suffered, she displayed many nervous traits. She had witnessed gun fire, burglaries, and murder. She had seen a shooting right in front of her one morning on the way to work. These experiences changed her personality, traumatising the very core of her being.

Whilst she was girly, elegant and often jumpy, she was good at her job. The staff training gave her a small measure of confidence, learning to walk tall she was chosen for most of the fashion shows, though she had an underlying edginess amongst her poise. Gunfire was uppermost in her mind; it could happen at any time. Hijacking and rape were never far from her thoughts, her memories would not let it go. She needed to stay vigilant at all times.

Jade never returned from a trip to Benoni to visit family. Anthea never saw her again or knew what had happened to her. There was no contact. Jade was sorely missed by Anthea in CaféB with the staff and customers always hoping her bubbly laugh would come bouncing through the doors in her usual controlled vigilant way.

Anthea's foot tapped like drum beats on the floor, as if she wanted her day to be rhythmic, definite, straight forward no beating about the bush. The ping-pong ball thoughts jiggled, having edged their way forwards for recognition. She thought often about Jade's story of the old steelyard she once worked at in a remote dusty town called *Olifantsfontein*, a small town with little in it of any interest. Transvaal, South Africa. It was Jade's nightmare. One morning she arrived at her work to find a death notice on her desk at the steel yard's office, where she was the secretary to the managing director. She was the only female in the entire steel yard.

Jade told Anthea how she spent every day wondering how her young child was coping with a black nanny, was her food being washed and bottle sterilised? Jade never knew why her child aged two had worms, tummy ache, the runs. A cold, runny nose continually dripping. One day Jade arrived home early and found the maid sleeping on the family room couch with the gardener. Naked, the two of them ran from the house, her child found in the cot, with three dirty bottles of milk.

Jade was a girl who saw the best in all people, was conscientious, a respectable worker and a lousy time keeper who loved to share deep feelings, though it was not always wise with whom she shared her thoughts and her memories which made Anthea's suitcase shudder, rattling the balls. Anthea had her own memories of similar experiences, while her coping mechanisms were healthy and firm, she gratefully appreciated her little brown suitcase, it was both a helper and a mystery in many ways. This was not the time or the place for these terrifying memories to jump their boundaries, wreck her day.

It was supposed to be a blissful morning, Anthea rummaged in her handbag for a pen. She believed bags had memories. She once found a fifty dollar note inside the zipped compartment of her preloved bag believing the memories left behind from the previous bag owner could interfere with her own. The relationship between a bag and owner were strong, until the contents of the bag outgrew the compartments.

She picked out a book for the morning from the elegant café bookshelf. Randomly opening it, she read a section on doing your best. She closed the book, mused on the subject she had read. It was perfect for her Christmas journey.

One day she might journey to that lowly 'Cattle Shed' the one that makes everything *Right….and no sadness was Left* '

Parts

Christmas came around more rapidly each year. Anthea had excited thoughts about the upcoming Ruth and Ken's Christmas show in a months' time. The relationships of the actors were both healthy and deeply rewarding while the makeup was still on. Behind the scenes, it was a different story. Many times, there were numerous insecurities going on between parts, between friend's and friend's parts. The boundaries of time and place strictly observed, Anthea felt those balls of humiliation starting to bump and jump, insecurities were gathering speed. Jealousy and Judgment Spring, winter, happy, sad. Decisions need good judgment; actions are open to wrong judgement and the critical views of others. Anthea chose not to go there at this moment, not this morning. She stayed in her happy place where her art collection and friends from the drama group were.

Ken and Ruth dropped in, they had been away on holiday and were welcomed back from their Scottish train trip through Great Britain. The trauma of life in Johannesburg sent them back to live in England.

While away in Britain, Ken and Ruth travelled the fifteen national parks throughout the British Isles. They were organising a film show of all the photos and stories from their trip.

Suggestions were that camping and sleeping bags, were to be arranged in the theatre hall. This would be a lengthy process, viewing the entire trip and Ruth was not one to cull any 'skerrick' of information. Cairngorms, Lake District and Snowdonia Wales.

New Forest and South Downs, of these, the South Downs and the Cairngorm Mountain range were Anthea's favourite places to take photographs and write her poetry.

Tiredness wafted over Anthea like a cloud over her own internal mountains. Some days, mountain tops with no rain, sometime storms across the range of her emotions. Any day the mayhem in London would start as crowds gathered in excitable clumps, bumping elbow to elbow, pushing and shoving, reaching for that last inflatable Rudolph and the *Saggy Santa Garden* ornament that will be swaying in the wind, in competition with the silver birch and bare willow trees.

The journey through tired nights, exhausting days, wild lunches, friend's break-ups, shop lifters, busy meetings at work. Fashion show, window dressing, washing clothes with fake snow stuck in the woollen fibres, late buses, broken down tubes, possible terror threats, writing Christmas cards, smiling at people you don't like, grumpy mothers, excitable children, traffic jams, baubles, and *Rudolph songs*, sung by every singer ever born, was utterly exhausting. Each year is the same. Nothing changes, it just becomes morefrantic every twelve months. By boxing day, her ears had heard too much Bing-Crosby. Her voice had lost the excitement tones, her enthusiasm for mince pies had waned considerably and all the boxing day sales commenced at dawn.

Room for doubt, self-doubt, judgement, uncertainties were things fought within her mind. Her thoughts wanted to air their voice, so did the judgment balls, the uncertainty balls, the indecision balls.

After deciding it could be a profitable exercise, she allowed the orderly formation of her opinions, hoping the balls would not challenge, which they inevitably did, with a nod of approval, like a major in the army, or ship's captain, the thoughts delivered their say.

'All any of us can do is our best. If it were true, we would do our best all the time' remembering Old Jacks frequent quote. Anthea smiled affectionately.

Judgement said we are all quite capable of doing our worst. Everything has opposites. There are plenty of times we believe we are doing our best, yet it turns out to be our worst, all this did for her was confirm room was needed for doubt, sometimes doubt can be right and helpful.

Enjoying her second cappuccino for the morning, she questioned the suitcase. Were the balls satisfied? she doubted, well doubt was happy he was not redundant. His department could not shut down. Doubt. Quite useful at times and Anthea considered the balls were almost human.

They reacted and spoke in a human way. It made Anthea hunt for more of the truth.

She had read the news headlines on the board by the paper stand on the corner of the street, stood to wonder if it was silly to encourage profound thoughts. She never saw adverts along the high street for discounted discussion classes on the meaning of life. 'People have given up asking that question,' she thought to herself under her breath. More useless headlines confronted her.

The Meaning of Life

The police had found a dead body in a rubbish tip, suspecting it was a missing woman from three weeks ago. Anthea winced as she considered the abuse many women suffered around these times.

Christmas, a highly stressful time of year, she understood her friend Jen was experiencing appalling abuse from her daughter Zoe.

There was nothing Anthea could do for now; all she could do

was to sip her long morning black with hot milk on the side. Indulge her senses in the artwork that surrounded her which hung from the walls of the cleverly designed café and hope for the best in the circumstances Jen was in.

CaféB her sanctuary, cleverly designed because from where she sat, she could see the courtyard garden with the large, ancient tree in the centre, standing out, proud like the centrepiece of any great country painting. The garden was surrounded by toughened glass to keep it as a centrepiece to the café rather than a wrecking ground for big and small feet, where she could watch the birds fly to and fro, sip the water, eat the seeds from the bird feeders hanging from the lower branch of the tree. The Blackbird, the Whistling Thrush, the Blue-tits, the Pigeons all came for a feed as she watched from her corner favourite seat.

Anthea also loved that she could view the entire collection of artworks from her cleverly designed corner. They were as varied, as eclectic as her personality, everything excited her mind.

Anthea loved the painting on the side wall of a strange tree. It was named Zebra Tree. It sat beside a huge clock. She remembered how interesting that was, painted by a young mother of two, there was a bit of a write up regarding this talented artist. Anthea treasured the fact Poges loved to support the local artists, no matter the style of art produced, everything from drama to paintings, costumes, books.

Pottery, other collectables, it all fitted inside the café snuggly. The garden had small pottery animals under the tree scattered around a small oak door built into the tree trunk. Poges called it the hobbit door. Inside the café near the gigantic clock were other paintings.

During the meeting for a coffee, an in-depth chat unravelled that morning. Anthea hoped there would be something in the conversation to bring realisation for Jen, help her face reality. Jen did not know how to best deal with it all and was at her wit's end.

Her intelligence and control of the situation had run dry, though she was a university lecturer of English literature, her mind told her she should cope. Jen put many expectations on herself to be a perfect mother, her problems were guilt-based, guilt that she worked long hours, full time, there was no answer to this problem. The mortgage had to be paid. Zoe was unfairly taking her frustrations out on Jen.

Jen was openly worried and beginning to suffer with continual indigestion and heart-burn. Was this indicative of the state of her own heart? wondered Anthea.

Judgment and the Jabiru

'Judgement, we all do it' thought Anthea, as she pulled the book she was reading from her bag.

Judgement, the Jabiru Jewel. 'It was a great read' she thought to herself. She thought about it a lot, as it had much in it to digest.

A Jabiru she discovered was an elegant type of stork found in Australia. It was a significant part of the book, gripping, poetic, unusual, Anthea liked it a lot. She loved birds, therefore loved reading books about birds remembering the Ibis bird was the weirdest looking bird on the planet, she had seen some strange birds over time. A Puffin is one of them.

Beautifully ugly, lives on the rugged cliffs of the Orkney Islands, Scotland.

Grande Production

Anthea belonged to a drama group in the past and had yearned to get back into it one day. That day had arrived months ago when Anthea met Ruth and Ken. after a successful advertising campaign, there were now some fresh creative actors becoming members.

Leigh, Suzanne, and Erin were all at CaféB. It was Saturday morning, all chatting about the opening night of the play.

The hour went fast and it was time to prepare for the production. Everyone in the team had responsibilities according to their talents.

Russell and Erin worked in the brewery that supplied CaféB and were placed in the lighting and costume department, Sondra, the producer was responsible for chair stacking.

Carlton the director he was the best at directing, even the floor washing after the show. Shane was directed to security and makeup. Anne, and Erin both from the historical society in Lambeth were front of house where they could chatter, eat, and laugh with the patrons while, showing them to their seats. Anne wrote the play and was also the prompt who mostly enjoyed sitting behind the curtains watching the actors bring her book to life.

"Murder by Candlestick"

The play was called *Murder by Candlestick*, about a vicar found dead in the grounds of the church. "Nothing new about that" said Poges as the frivolity and laughter increased around the table. 'Did everyone have a living breathing table?'

Anthea wondered 'or was it just unique to table31 swallowing up the words of every conversation'. Kevin who ran the photography department at Harrods and forever had a camera on his shoulders, arrived earlier that morning to set up the camera positions ready to film the play before everyone arrived.

Emily was delivering the artwork needed for front of house and the stage during the interval. Josephina was a bit late delivering the costumes that she had to fix up that week, Ruth was anxious as usual that the props would be ready on time.

"Did anyone find the missing candlestick"? Ruth yelled across the café in a high-pitched voice, "Ask Shane" replied Poges over the noise at the café and the laughter grew.

Katya threw up her hands and laughed saying …"Great I do have something to report on now." And was also playing the part of the reporter on the murder case. Poges made sure he was in the front seat of the audience that night. He supplied the coffee and champagne after the show to celebrate opening night with the cast.

Georgina who was very gifted in cutting and chopping WOOD…and banging in nails… created the set for the production.

"We will see what that's like" yelled out Ken *after* she admitted she ran out of lighting during the electrical failure a few nights earlier.

Georgina admitted she had borrowed the Candlestick for a dinner party she was holding at her home.

When her large German Shepherd sat on it and chewed it like a bone, she had to quickly make another one as a replacement before anyone realised it was missing used the large antique candlestick and forgot to put it back in the props room. "Oh, the joys of local theatre" rang out from the dressing room. Remembering it was still in her car; Georgina promised to get it to the theatre early.

Ken played the Vicar and yelled out across the café "Remember to put the blood on it George" he shouted, as Georgina tossed a glare at him….was that real blood Ken? Thinking out loud, Ken laughed at the theatrics of it all.

Everything went smoothly, the first night was a wonderful success. Katya reported the successful night and was splashed across the London papers. This was a big deal for the city. Nothing thrilled Anthea more than seeing those characters work within the boundaries of their words, unite in accord of the one product.

The Grande production was brilliant. The show went on for several more nights. It was good business for Poges and CaféB as Poges did a dinner theatre transport package.

Mrs Buttons

After work each night, Anthea enjoyed relaxation time, researching her bird books, as usual, she sat in her 22nd-floor apartment with incredible views from the window overlooking Hyde Park.

Anthea felt at home overlooking the place she used to go rowing with her first love, Bob Buttons. However, her father forbade that relationship, as the families were polar opposites in the political world. "Never mix politics and pleasure" she said to herself, smiling on her way to bed.

The weather had changed overnight, typical for this time of year, or for that matter, any time of year. The perfume in the trains had changed too. Boots and furs that smelt of moth balls as she sat on the tube that hummed as it raced through tunnels under busy London.

Anthea adored the busy, noisy city life most times. Her choice of living, her choice of life and choice of nurturing her soul was to sit and ponder the outside world where there were hundreds of people and nobody knew one another.

All total strangers, all needing to have that first intake of caffeine.

'No wonder the world was a lonely planet, people were disconnected, too busy and too tired to do anything about it' she thought. Anthea had created an inside world of varying degrees of emotions. It helped with the loneliness of city life.

That was the job of the little brown suitcase, to organise her emotions, keep the ping-pong balls in order.

Most times, her soul was as happy as a bee on a *Juniper flower*. When the suitcase was happy, Anthea was the bee. She loved Junipers, the name, the fragrance, the colours made her feel contented inside. The absolute opposite of the small village, where her primary school years were spent, inside her old historic red-bricked school though there were many similarities.

There was a small garden with Junipers and history was evident all around the building. At that moment a loud screeching of tyres and beeping horns made her jump, as a van marked *pest control* squeezed in front of a number 31 bus. "Oh, rats" she shuddered the words from her mouth as a memory jumped out from nowhere. 'My small primary school was full of rats, jumping past the water tanks high up in the ceiling.' She would count them like sheep in her sleep, counting one, two, three as they jumped and cleared the gap past the exposed water tank, clearly un-beknown to the teacher.

When Anthea was disinterested in the fractions and trigonometry, counting rats was better than adding up rows of numbers like her dad. Rats were never boring, reminding her of the history of London, the rats, the plague.

She wondered some days if her teacher had the plague as she bent over Johnathon's table to mark his books, taking a little longer than usual.

Anthea saw her large grandma knickerbockers once and definitely thought she had the plague.

Junipers Shame

Anthea was in deep thought regarding relationships, cautiously aware of triggering those wretched ping-pong balls, throwing her off the beaten track. She wondered about this life and the involvements 'Mr may I borrow your salt man' had endured. Our experiences make us who we are. Anthea sat for a while, wondering how many genuine smiles he had generously given in his life? and not the ones that ensured he got something in return. His mother, his father, had they been the same to him? Programmed, formed into his father's image? Was it learned behaviour?

Anthea wanted to find out the sad truth behind this person. Was a smile an emotion? or was it a smart cover over a deep sadness, a clown heavily made up with a caked-on cosmetic mask. Had there been a time in his life that had stolen his smile? She gave him the name because the only thing he had ever said in the several years she had seen him at the CaféB, was *may I borrow your salt* man. He spoke on the phone at length to intelligent people, strange thing, his table never had salt on it.

Table Salt

One morning, Anthea devised a plan. Arriving earlier than normal, though she rarely had *normal* in her life, she put a salt shaker on his usual table.

He arrived and sat at a different table, with no salt.

The situation became curiouser and curiouser, Anthea quoted a line from her favourite story from the children's book *Alice in wonderland*. Her mind always darted to and fro, from book to book like a bee on a thistle, knowing that one day she would write her first book. Perhaps calling it 'The table with no salt' she thought. It would be a thriller, with a little drama, a bit other worldish and a 'who dun-it' thrown into the mix of genre. Typically, eclectic and off the beaten track, it would have to be a best seller.

The following day Anthea asked Poges how well he really *knew* the tall grey-haired man. Poges said he did not reply "there are people you know and people you know well Anthea" he said, while juggling the beer tumblers in threes. She asked him if he could make sure there was salt on every table, Poges laughed all the way to the kitchen. Mr Salt man did not arrive that day. Anthea gave up. She wondered if she would constantly have infuriating people in her life.

In dashed her old school friend JJ, short for Johnathon Jenkins who also remembered the school teachers' knickerbockers, yet could not remember her name. He was with his favourite cousin Juniper. She had secured a career as a forensic scientist and thoroughly enjoyed the mystery behind every working day. Anthea welcomed them with a warm hug and a carefully delivered smile. He talked as if he was speed dating and was permanently busy on the phone.

His raucous Scottish accent was fun, though ridiculously tricky to understand, Anthea called that an earphones day.

Once they had gone past the preliminaries, first "how was your family?" followed by "what was the weather doing, did you bring a coat?" then discussing whether the planets were all in alignment for the day, followed by the newspaper headlines, which were down the line of importance. The next hour was plain boring.

Anthea had an accent headache. She got it often when too many accents were in the same room.

Juniper however, was fascinating to listen to. Anthea loved all the stories she heard; it constantly filled her head with what she called *Novel Fodder*. The newspapers were full of information about the world which also provided more good stories.

The latest news that Juniper had to share around at table 31 was that her brother Simon, who was a captain on a ship, a notable royal cruise liner, was caught entertaining a group of Japanese in his cabin. Juniper had always felt so proud of her brother, delighted he had achieved such great honour to captain a notable ship, proud he had worked hard for his outstanding achievements in life. She loved to drop his name into most conversations and Juniper became known as a 'name dropper.'

Simon mixed with famous people from all around the world. "I'm hobnobbing with the rich and famous" he always reminded his sister; she was happy for him and felt special around him. "Nothing wrong with feeling proud" she used to say to Anthea, to anyone who heard her. Juniper's pride was about to crumble.

There were many people who were jealous of the happiness, contentment and joys of life that surrounded her. Her days were always bright and cheerful, she had many friends and was genuinely at peace with the world. The newspaper article she had just read, crushed her joy, and let the jealous demon have free run to turn her dancing into mourning, turning her joy to shame around the table. There was laughter and sniggers and Juniper felt all sense of respect had just slid under the table.

Simon had set the ship to cruise control, while attending a private function in his quarters and was subsequently caught having a shiatsu massage when his pager beeped furiously. Julian his second in command had rushed to find him, discovering he had his pants down while there was an out-of-control fire in the galley and was too busy to smell the smoke filtering through the air or under the doors. There was chaos and panic and of course the investigations, the latest news was he had been marched from the ship leaving the cruise line to deal with the aftermath.

Juniper was mortified, as she has always spoken proudly of her brother. Now everyone knew the story, she had retreated into a shell, secluded herself for a while and was rarely seen in company, while everyone was talking about it.

One or two people mentioned they had not seen Juniper since that newspaper disclosed the truth of the matter.

Anthea wondered about the reasons people felt embarrassed at someone else's mistakes or crimes. It was not Juniper's fault, yet she expressed horror and embarrassment about the news as she was connected by genetics and family name.

Simon worked with a friend Reginald who had his eye on promotion, heading for captaincy if there was a place available. Reginald was a go getter, climbing to the top position in any job he had and was never satisfied until he reached the top. He was willing to step on anyone or anything to get there. He broke up marriages and families if it meant the top job was his.

He worked under the radar, having no empathy for the trauma he caused in getting the top seat. Blonde hair, blue eyed, suave, he held everyone's attention whenever he had the opportunity. A *"Steve McQueen* look alike" everyone said. Reginald was a Jealous man by nature and hid it well by being kind. "Kindness with an agenda"

Simon always said, though they were best of friends, Simon knew kindness came with expectations, Reginald needed

Simon to jump ship so to speak so he could rise up the ladder, get another foot on the career path. 'Jealousy causes many a catastrophe' thought Anthea, as she heard the heart wrenching account of Junipers outpouring. Many thoughts appeared one after another as Anthea jumped from one opinion to another remaking the story, each take with a different ending.

Simon was facing a harrowing few months and it would be hard to explain why a massage was necessary on his watch. Anthea believed there was more to it than Juniper disclosed. Time, truth, and knowledge would unravel the understanding needed for Juniper's healing as she was spiralling into shame she did not own, neither should she carry.

Jealousy and workplace bullying were the hidden virus of the shop floor. It was prevalent in every workplace, every shop floor Anthea has ever worked in. It was tiring to be in continual, watchful, suspicion of colleagues who were plotting to push you out, or anyone who got in the way of 'their' agendas. Anthea was determined to succeed in overcoming bullies in the work place.

Though never easy and often covert, she enjoyed the challenge of discovering how bullies hide their agendas.

Anthea had changed jobs. For the past year, her days filled with fashion, colour, fun, pressure, deadlines, fabrics, patterns, excited people, she was part of it all. Having worked in a different department within the House of Fraser group it was reasonably easy to move around the various departments after the initial twelve months.

Anthea felt saddened and was deeply affected by the terrible story of Junipers' only family member and supported her through many months of awaiting an outcome. The subject of choices was uppermost in her mind. 'If you make a wrong decision, it affects your entire life. That is the scariest problem we all need to deal with.'

Anthea thought about choices all day. Her aunt made a wrong choice of husbands three times affecting all five of her children's lives in many different ways.

Even the Queen had to decide as to which jar of marmalade her coat of arms would be attached to, if only life was that simple, choices and decisions. A lot of people love the Royal family because she gives guidance and leadership and has done so all her life. People love her for the stability and values she gives everyday people in all walks of life, She is a normal person born into a tribe. The coat of arms is the family crest the Queen uses to stamp her approval onto products she trusts.

Anthea's mother would buy any product that had her stamp of approval. This raised another thought for Anthea, the big subject of 'Trust.' What happens if the Queen's family falls apart, like her aunt's family? What happens to trust then? Do you throw out the jar of marmalade?

Coat of Arms

The Queen's coat of arms was something Anthea's mother was proud of as if it were her own. Seen almost everywhere throughout London, it was a familiar sight. Back in the early days of her childhood home, her father's marmalade jar and the two jam jars had the coat of arms on it to show the Queen's approval, a stamp of her own.

Anything from Harrods had her stamp; postage stamps always had her head on them, as did every school in the country of the Commonwealth.

Australia included. Law courts had the Royal coat of arms blazoned above the doorways.

Anthea enjoyed seeing letters with the Royal coat of arms sometimes drop on the floor of her family home *Harali*, by the front door with the big white netting curtain that fluttered in the draught as the letters were pushed through the post flap. A gust of wind blew the envelope from the House of Fraser onto the hallway floor.

The arrival of the letter when Anthea was just twenty meant she was part of the Harrods group of stores. How exciting to be chosen to be a part of England's most famous store. This scenario made her feel approved of. At last, she would have the approval of her parents and the little brown suitcase would be healed, happy and fulfilled.

Anthea relished with pride the new challenges that came with the job. She loved the new relationships and people in her life. Over the years, she moved through the ranks and became the personnel officer, hiring and firing and training new recruits. Having trained many new faces, some of whom went on to become managers.

Josefina was Anthea's new trainee, the latest member of the team as a trainee fashion designer, although a little bit of a challenge with her thoughts on uniforms. She was not keen to be confined to a uniform she disliked the colour of.

Josefina came from the Balearic Islands off Spain, with long, dark wavy hair, she had a fun personality and loved all her work. In fact, she was happy in most jobs she had. However, in the short period of time during her training, she had been saying this job was "her worst nightmare."

Stuck in a shop, behind glass windows being watched by passers-by, children banging on the window and pulling faces at her, Josefina wanted to cover the window with black paper.

Scatty in the areas of paperwork, she would often draw amusing cartoons on her sales slips, which depicted the character of the customers and clients, many of whom purchased hundreds of thousands of pounds worth of dresses for their Arabian harems. This became a problem when a high-end Sheik noticed the caricature of himself, as Josefina had left the desk momentarily to collect one of the dresses that was left hanging inside a changing room. She tried justifying herself by explaining it was a cartoon of another staff member. However, it was clear no other staff member wore a sheet in the shape of an origami camel on their head.

Wrong Choice

Josefina's position did not last long as this young trainee brought in a kind of country, outback, cowgirl appearance with the horsey touch to her designs. Though the Queen loved horses, it was not the elegant upper-class style befitting the Harrods showroom. The fashion could have been trendy; however, this bubbly fun-loving, good-natured young girl often dressed the windows in mud, straw and goodness knows what other props the paddocks had deposited on the floor from her boots. This fashion did not go down well with the Harrods establishment. Sadly,

Josefina was ushered into the office and dismissed for having stepped outside the regimental lines at Harrods.

The head of the department insisted on calling her "Josephine" and often yelled it across the shop floor, echoing her extreme annoyance. She never finished her three months' probation and permanently left work that afternoon by horse and carriage after a group of her friends had arranged a classy getaway for her. People smiled as word got around, truly understanding and nodding in approval of the slightly rebellious young girl testing all the outrageous boundaries possible. Harrods was not the place to do it.

Josefina went on to Tintagel, Cornwall, to live and work with rescued horses on a farm in a disused coalmine. The farm was often used to make movies, like *Poldark*. She was perfect for the job and the star of the town after she played a part in a movie about a horse that became stuck inside a mine shaft. Anthea's brain loved these happy ping-pong memories.

Shamed

Coffee and the weekend newspapers, *Broadway* playing on the stereo, Poges jiggling, dancing and generally being Irish was the essence of CaféB life. Everything about the café enhanced Anthea's journey through life. The girls enjoyed good music, great conversation and chewing over the news.

Juniper quickly turned from relaxed to fraught in an instant as they gnawed over the day's headlines. The original intention was to light-heartedly sip, laugh, and dissect the papers, but was lost as they both read the full article on, *Ship's Captain Shamed in Shiatzu Shemozzle.*

Tears rolled down Juniper's face as she read the full article on her brother. Her pride was totally shattered, as was all hope, as she fought to fight back shame and the fear of laughter, of not-so-nice friends that surrounded her once she arrived at work, knowing that everyone knew.

She also had jealousy all around her as friends wanted to see her slip up. She held her head up and fought back the grip shame had on her chest. Simon had been set up by Reginald to take the massage and keep the guests happy, while Reginald took care of the deck. Simon had suffered terrible back pain and took the idea of a massage willingly. Reginald visited the galley to check out the progress of the banquet planned for the high-class Japanese guests. Starting the fire himself, he created the furore as the emergency unfolded, gas exploded in the galley creating an inferno. Where was the captain? Reginald, who was planning his next few steps up the ladder at Simon's expense, fell from a great height, as did Simon. They both drank from the same cup, but from different sides.

"Life is change. Growth is optional. Choose wisely."
[Simons favourite quote.]

Table 31. You are my favourite distraction. You help my decisions, allowing me protection from my weariness and oppositions. You fill my cup.

K

CHAPTER 11

Knowledge Kingdom Rules Katy and Producer Ken

Anthea and Katy met at the CaféB to discuss merchandising and an advertising program for the latest fashion show. That was a fun part of the job for both of them. The discussion involved looking at colour schemes and all that goes with selling products from the show. The discussion together opened up a conversation on fake news. Katy was writing an article about that subject as she despised fake news and wanted to interview one or two people at the café while she was there. "No fake news here," Poges laughed.

Most times Katy enjoyed her job; however, it lacked the fun side, and she was looking to expand her experiences into the wider world outside reporting the news and London fashion shows. Though her name originated from Russia, she did prefer the English version, Katy. She used to work at the Kremlin, reporting things that were all well and good, perfect in the world, at the embassy. Let's say, they portrayed a 'perfect' society through controlled media. Thus, 'Katya' in the news was just Katy to her friends. She loved both hats. Friendships and fame.

Having just secured the top headlines around the world from the article she wrote on the ship's captain and the entire *massage* episode, her name shot to fame as millions had read the story.

Knowledge, truth, and insight prepared her as a sought-after reporter. This international story caused her house phone to be ringing all week.

The Times, Reuters, and London's Daily Mail all offered a contract for her to join them.

Expanding Knowledge

For work she had her standard smart fashions in her preferred colours spilling out of her designer wardrobe. She looked for colours that gave her confidence, what she called optimistic tones.

Bright and cheery. Red lipstick was the new season's colour. At weekends, Katy loved nothing better than slopping around in her baggy trackpants, floppy shirts and flat shoes, no jewellery, and a clean face.

Red lipstick, a passion for truth and knowledge in her line of work, it was her trump card. Knowledge and answers were both vital, necessary, whether for news, or for skincare.

Every word had to matter as long as it conveys the true meanings and carries, the message. This was the essence of intelligent conversation.

Meeting up with her friend Anthea for coffee always promised interesting conversations.

Still on the hunt for clues, knowledge was crucial for finding the solutions to the name *Harali* and its connection with the Isle of Wight. The stickers Anthea saw in her dreams on the little brown suitcase were part of the puzzle to solve its relevance to her family history. 'Knowledge working hand in hand with understanding could solve all the world's problems,' she thought.

Anthea had recently bought herself a gorgeous steel grey woollen cape, it was stunning.

The wool hung heavily, swung left and right as she walked elegantly across the road. She felt a million eyes were on her, making her feel elegant like a Hollywood film star. Her mother liked the cape, it was quite unusual to get approval from her mother. Having cool afternoon winds and chilled nights, the cape would be well used for the next several months. She remembered one she had as a child age five, same colour.

The Revlon counter was always popular, neat, clean, well-organised and it was Anthea's responsibility to keep it organised and train the new staff members in sales of cosmetics, she enjoyed wearing the grey and burgundy uniform. Uniforms were a symbol of pride and whilst many of her friends refused to have work that involved a uniform, Anthea relished the unity and sense of belonging it gave her.

All the lipsticks were displayed in colour order according to the rainbow. Reds first, with violets on the end of the mirrored metallic display case. She enjoyed having new opportunities and she was quickly able to transfer from Harrods to Selfridges, Oxford Street, without much effort.

Harrods training school was beneficial, it was where she gained knowledge of more advanced cosmetics and French perfumes.

After a couple of years, Anthea took the plunge and opened her own business in hair, beauty and cosmetics and pretty soon opened her own beauty clinic in Sussex, south of London, in a little town called Shoreham by the Sea.

She spent less time in London and built up a lucrative business at the foothills of the South downs. Katy was multi-talented and had created her own skincare range, so they complemented each other. Anthea supplied Harrods and brought her skincare range into Anthea's salon. Katy could mix *news reporting* easily with her skincare business.

Regular travel over to the continent, Rome, Milan, and Paris was going to be inspiring. Life looked idyllic; life looked exciting for Katy.

Mingling with the rich and famous each day, Asian, Middle Eastern people from many philosophies came into Selfridges. Dozens of Arabs arrived each day to buy perfumes for their many wives in Arabia from this prestigious London store. Katy loved the mix of Europeans and Americans, she took in some deep, steady breaths as she watched people coming in, going out.

Journalism was easy as she travelled and the skincare range just blended into the spare hours in-between. Katy was meeting up with Anthea, along with a couple of work colleagues to discuss some details on the reviews she was doing in her publication for fashion around London.

Noticing CaféB had been freshly painted, Poges did a great job keeping the café in tip-top condition. Anthea loved the way Poges changed the paintings from time to time. There were fresh ones, old ones, modern ones, 'Constable,'

'Monet,' 'Picasso,' such a variety. It seemed that once Anthea received the message she needed, Poges who was unaware of this mystery, changed the painting. Sometimes it could take months.

This month's painting was John Constable. 'The Hay Wain' painted in 1821.

John died on the thirty first of march 1837 of heart failure. She knows this because she loves to learn about the *Artist* as well as the painting.

What message Anthea received from this painting was yet to be found. Painted in the setting of the river Stour, Flatford, Suffolk. Another famous part of Constable's collection 'Flatford Mill' and 'Hadleigh Castle' where many a school holiday was spent with picnics, her mother, the siblings and the neighbours Joan, Caroline and Robin and most times Valentina, that was the community. Hadleigh Castle was in ruins; however, it was so much fun to play hide and seek. Anthea knew there was both connections and messages in this painting of the cart pulling a heap of hay. Thinking it was deeper than the fact that she loved both the smell, the feel, and the sight of hay because "hay" meant horses... she spoke out load. She knew it must go deeper; she must also learn patience.

Memories of Valentina were sweet, extremely special and above all they remained like sisters. Valentina's mother Edith, was the *aunty* Anthea wanted and adored. They lived next door to *Harali*. Edith used to chase the girls round and round the garden, jumping over rose bushes and past the washing line prop, up the gravel driveway until both girls and herself were all exhausted.

Those were days when one day felt like a thousand years. These days, a year feels like an hour. Edith was a very special part of Anthea's life as was Valentina. The family moved away when Anthea was fourteen to live on the Isle of wight.

Time Is Awkward

The fun time seemed to last for hours, then it was time for home-made lemonade in the kitchen before Anthea headed home. That meant climbing under the garden fence and all before dark, and before her father arrived home. Anthea was terrified of catching sight of the flared nostrils and stern look of disapproval. 'Aunty' as she was called, Edith always made sure it rarely happened.

Shared childhood experiences from all the girls made coffee time mostly filled with laughter, as everyone related with additions to each story.

Time zipped by and the girls made their arrangements for the coming weekend. Katy asked Anthea many questions regarding her choice of café, why did she choose it and why did she only ever go to the one same café? commenting on what a great find it was. The reason was that Anthea adored the unusual arty things dotted around. She excitedly told Katy about the encounters within her soul that occur, she once seen a painting on the wall with a disappearing pathway that went past bushes on a beach and knew it meant her path was about to change and there was a secret, she did not know the answer to yet. Once she turned her corner, she would find it out, discovering what the next stage in her life was, or the answer to the burning question within her thoughts. Where was she going, what direction would her life take.

She had thoughts and messages given to her when they were

most needed, whether through the paintings, or a small note left on the table by mistake, or serendipitous. She carried on with her examples and how chance can change your life, as can pre-determined. It's one of those conversations that get nowhere. The vibrations that she often felt at the table were similar to a small earth tremor. It was extraordinary and quite unexplainable how the table was continually free, or someone was leaving as she arrived. The timing could not be a coincidence, she was meant to be there. The table was going to reveal something to her, as the quest for knowledge never stopped.

Table 31 inspired thought, revealed choices, doors, keys through old wooden things, flowers, artefacts even the clock which she coveted. Anthea glanced at the clock; it seemed to have stood still. Sometimes an hour could seem like a day or a year, depending on where her head was going. Today it seemed like the length of a year, much was going on in her mind. She was relieved table31 could contain her emotions the way she needed it.

The Bookshelf Anthea had finished a book and always wondered how the title was born, this book was called *Fair Stood the Wind for France*. The title was the drawcard for her, anything about France caught her attention. Having read the book at school twenty years earlier she had forgotten most of the story. Reading a second time around always brought a valuable new insight.

She found time each morning on the train and relished that hour and enjoyed the journey the book took her on. She loved a book with a great ending which this one did, making her cry, the emotion dripped from her nose, somewhat embarrassing on a train. After all the effort put into reading it, she was sad to close the cover. Anthea stared out of the dirty windows, watching the queued traffic and relishing the ending of her book as if she did not want to let it go. The story was of a Jewish girl during the end of World War 2, who had been protected from being rounded up for the concentration camps. The story went on to talk about her love for France and her love for one of the soldiers who had protected her by hiding her under floor boards. It was a true story and had been adapted into a movie.

From the carriage windows, Anthea could see old buildings speeding past as the train neared the end of the journey towards *Liverpool Street Station*. Buildings blackened with soot from chimneys, which held many stories between the walls. Many that might have been long lost love stories. Her mind relished those feelings of her own first love at school, during the time of her first reading this book. She remembered how that felt, never knowing how chance and destiny played a part in her future. If that knowledge was hers back in her school days, her choices may have been different.

The book rested back on the café bookshelf ready for the next reader. Though she felt sad to let it go, Anthea was excited about the next read. Usually, picking the books with the hardcovers, or the ones with the old red covers she took time

checking the latest arrivals of donated books. Like a lucky dip at a church fete, her childlike excitement grew.

She liked to be transported back to her school days when most books seemed to have red covers, as did this new book she pulled off the shelf. On the front cover it had an arrangement of kangaroo paws in a vase on a table which looked like a rickety old farmhouse. Anthea wondered what they were, as she had never heard of 'putting kangaroo paws in a vase.' For a vegan, this was not a pleasant thought at all, indeed not in London.

The book was set in outback Australia where there are no knights, kings, a kingdom, or castles, draw bridges or swords. The only knight she knew was the one on her chessboard. Anthea was fascinated by the thought of the Australian outback. The horses, cattle, the dogs were red, as was the earth, with colours resembling sunsets, also the horrors of drought, horrors of fires. This book sounded different and fascinating, she took it home and began her new journey into the outback.

Kangaroo Paw Valley

The concepts that appealed to Anthea that ran through the book, were *Trust and Safety*. Anthea was already relating to the feelings from page one.

Though the setting was very different to any personal experience, she felt as if she were there. Having always wanted to run a farm the story was thoroughly engaging.

The heroine was called Kitty. The book delved into the knowledge Kitty needed to run a farm, to live a full life in the outback. Kitty loved her cowgirl skirts, being the kind of girl Anthea would love to have been or to have as a friend.

Surrounded by farming machinery, sheds, the smells of hay. She wondered how people did their washing up in those days, the type of soap they had. Those long khaki skirts needed to be washed until all the red earth around the hems were removed.

She became excited when reading about the birds, particularly the Kestrel, Kite, and most of all the Kookaburra. The gum trees, the tricky, sneaky snakes thrilled her imagination about Australia. Imagine walking through rainforests at dawn and looking up at those enormous trees, knowing some ankle biting creature was hidden, or setting off raucous laughter going on in the woods at daybreak. 'A delightful place that must be,' thought Anthea as she gazed back to the garden at CaféB, noticing through the glass window, Poges had created a scene with a pond, a swooping Kingfisher, and a new sign.

Goodness knows where he would have found a Kingfisher made of pottery and beautifully painted. Poges noticed her looking at his new creation, threw his hands out in a manner saying "Yes, I'm very clever and talented." Laughing, he continued making up the coffee orders.

Anthea looked down at her chosen attire for the day. Not nearly as exciting as a long khaki skirt with a red earth smeared hem, though she did enjoy the garden window Poges had created, a fairy glen of water birds, the bird feeder table with warbling thrushes. She loved London yet yearned for the life of the Australian outback; she was equally torn between the two, although she imagined she could not cope full-time with all the dust, flies and lack of water that came with outback Australia. How would the little brown suitcase cope with the severe experiences of a new country?

Anarchy in the suitcase, the awkward subject on how to keep her ping-pong balls under control, was getting harder. Anthea's mind was focused on the revelation knowledge brings, realising that once she'd received the knowledge, it opened ability to act. 'How does knowledge look?' It was not complicated the voice in her mind told her. Many balls became disapproving, critical, judgmental. Others were excited at the thought of no longer being prisoner, captive inside an ancient crabby old suitcase, while some balls simply liked their home. Rules within the case must remain rules, not guidelines, plain rules. Crossing borders was not a rule to be broken.

Anthea wanted to open the lid and let the balls run riot, into freedom. This was impossible when they had not acquired the wisdom to handle the freedom. Her thoughts could not yet be set free. This was why she often had headaches.

Anarchy in the suitcase caused her violent headaches, whereby she needed to go home and sleep. 'Perhaps if I disregard them, they will go away. Or if I throw the rule book at them, throw away the key, shut the door, build a brick wall, anything but listen to the rioting within.' Anthea cried out for the answer.

Looking up at the wall of art, she stared deeply into the space between the wall and the painting. Her eyes wide open yet glazed, allowing time to reveal what it needed.

Noticing a poster Poges had put up that morning that had a message somewhere for her.

It was a painting of all the artists and musicians from the nineteenth century.

Beethoven, Gershwin, Cole Porter, and Chopin. What a delightful poster, she could see Vincent VanGogh's 1889 *Starry Night*, Da Vinci and his Mona Lisa, his Last Supper from 1498, the beautiful *Girl with a Pearl Earring* by

Johannes Vermeer 1665 and the words 'Get to know them'. That was critical for their healing. Their freedom, the balls needed a voice to be heard. How else did they become prisoners? The balls were prisoners because they were misunderstood and had no voice. They were not allowed to express emotions.

Anthea decided to start with why they were the colour they were. How did the colours appear? They help her order her thoughts by colour. Red ping-pong balls were the rebellious ones. Usually, 'little suitcase' had one red ball, yet they seemed to be breeding. Now, four red balls appeared and agitated the others. The pink ball was labelled *'precise.'*

Kingdom Keeper

If Anthea's day was not going precisely to plan, it caused ructions in the red department, the pink balls were unhappy. Thus, a well-ordered day was advisable to keep her tightly guarded mind at ease. Next were the orange balls, they want a routine day to relax. Orange for ordinary order. Orderly line ups, no boundary jumping. No queue jumping. The yellow balls were the shy, nervous, cowardly ones who don't have courage. They jump boundaries to get out of the way from the friction within. Cowardly, fearful. Yellow balls carry excessive weight, stress. The balls labelled green were envious of any other balls. The green ones were jealous, envious whistle-blowers. Don't rattle the greens. Blue balls were the bullies.

Anthea had a headache. An unhappy cerebellum was not a great feeling.

Every department had a bully. Bullies coerce others to gain

ground, bribe covertly manipulating more balls to join them. Every office had one. A bully. Surviving the covert control of one was tiring, often leaving Anthea exhausted by the end of the day.

Wait, there were two more compartments, one labelled infringement, which meant the case needed a judgement department, an injustice department, and the lawmakers. The judges checked if the other balls had breached the contract, which most times they had. By jumping a boundary or mixing compartments, dabbling in the affairs of different departments or any other unsettling behaviour assures the infringement balls had the last say. They trump all other balls.

The last in the regiments of ping-pong balls were labelled *Violet Voyeur*, the watchers. The gatekeepers, who attend all the activities going on inside her head.

The internal systems had a strict duty to report to the chief of staff, the chairperson, or in this case, the little-brown suitcase. While the balls were all white, Anthea would have a great day, if not, her PTSD was triggered, the rainbow of nervous activities, anxieties commenced.

White was good, rainbow was not. Mixing balls within communities of the mind was unwise, there was no wisdom in it. Knowledge within Anthea's mind proved to be more beneficial than she imagined. There was one other ball, the

cynical black ball. However, there was a long way to go to succeed in her quest to find meaning to the stickers in her dream on the little brown suitcase.

A previous conversation that started as a quiet observation

within her mind, during Anthea's reading of the morning papers. The article was of the riots that had gone wild in various large cities around the world. Thoughts became riots in her mind which employed the black ball or cynical ball. It soon gets out of control and Anthea needs to bring order into the suitcase somehow. Mixing cultures together in communities. An excellent idea. Mingling all nationalities together, each losing their identities and traditions, they get lost. They can't function. The boundaries won't let those balls mix. They cannot get passed the *no ability to blend* boundary.

It is the same system as in Europe.

Passports are needed to cross from Italy and France, the little suitcase is no different.

Everybody's mind had a *passport control* deep inside. Poges turned the music up, which began playing in the background. Cole Porter "Don't Fence Me in" a message for the suitcase maybe?

Other Cultures

'Who thought up this idea?' wondered Anthea. This problem idea, too many examples of races, cultures, ethics, spiritual, traditional worldwide nations all coming together.

Many kinds of jumbled mixtures of tribal, cultural lives that try to mingle with the 'Western' philosophies of the day. 'Political thought police abound' believed Anthea. Her thoughts were kept tightly and safely in the suitcase. Nobody knew the balls were crossing boundaries. Yet they were, and feeling undetected and safe, they were able to cause trouble in even the strongest mind.

Table 31, was the only place where all her balls were known. Friends knew they were safe when discussing the day's topics. The news headlines, the current affairs at Westminster. Safety at table31 was where you don't have to be politically correct for the times. For now.

From Russia with Love

It was a cold November the 11th morning, Katy was reporting at the dawn service, *Armistice Day.*

She wanted freedom, truth and needed to come west to find it and was considering a career change. Perhaps something more adventurous and become a travel writer. Having mastered the English language, she wanted to promote Japan in an English magazine.

Having always thought travel would be fun, she moved to Kyoto in Japan, but having been through the Eastern bloc, she quickly became homesick and realised she was not suited to this job at all. Anthea, certain that it would be short lived, watched, and waited. Katy changed jobs like she did her face creams and as fast as the news changed.

During her visit to Japan, writing an article on Temples and the Bamboo Forest, Katy realized her truth. Travelling the world sounded glamourous but it was exhausting. Jetlag and changing foods were bad for the skin in her view, not healthy. Lack of sleep and changing time zones were conducive to ill health. Although Katy loved the bamboo forest and was a lover of fish, the food was a weakness for her. She enjoyed the temples, the unfamiliar ethos like taking shoes off, sitting on the floor when eating and super-fast bullet trains. How clean it was compared to the dirt in London streets where overflowing bins of rubbish is spread around by the millions of pigeons.

Kyoto was impeccable, the stations were spotless, no train graffiti or doodles allowed, no chewing gum on the pavements, manners were perfect, the train ticket inspectors bow to the passengers as they enter and leave for the next carriage. Katy was impressed, she loved her life and her job was an education but homesickness caused her depression. She spent several months in Japan.

Returning to London

Katy had to find her own philosophy on life and settle into a comfortable place she called home, a place where she fitted. The first thing she did when moving back into a flat was fly the Union Jack from a flagpole outside her lounge room window. Passers-by often heard the music from 'Land of Hope and Glory' blaring from behind her double-glazed windows.

Upon returning to London Anthea and Poges welcomed her back and were so glad to see her and hear all her experiences. Anthea laughed each time Katy bowed her head after their time together. Poges laughed and thought it was rather cute. Living back in London, Kensington, with beautiful gardens and parks. However, Katy had to re-acquaint herself with chewing gum, rubbish, overfilled bins, graffiti of every gross kind imaginable. She had to make the choice of freedom and truth, or culture and a facade that everything was well in her life. It was not. It is not for the faint-hearted to move around the world, to mix cultures, to change your own philosophies on life.

Her new flat was not far from the impressive Science Museum and the Victoria and Albert Museum. She had plenty of work reporting on the Royal family, plus the enjoyment of growing her skincare products. She handled a busy life well considering multi-tasking was her energy supply.

There was regular scrambling between journalists for news of weddings, babies, and 'Royalty' in this part of London. Katy fostered enough self-confidence to wear all the beautiful, elegant clothes she bought from Harrods. She loved the job because it delivered a variety of assignments and was good at it. Her latest work was to promote Selfridges, London's most popular department stores to the world.

Katy and Anthea held their meetings at CaféB. They liked the complimentary glass of wine, Poges sense of humour and the energy at Table 31. Some weeks they worked together on the various cosmetics counters, promoting new skincare ranges in Vogue, Vanity Fair, and other quality magazines. Royal antics and skincare were Katy's favourite subjects. She had a contented life. Finding the keys of knowledge enabled her to find the satisfaction life had to offer.

Keys of Knowledge

Keys were answers well-hidden, yet obvious when found. The world needed answers to reasons why drama, or trauma happen in the lives of people.

The reasons why there were unexplained deaths or suicides or violence in a world that prayed for peace or expected peace, love, all good things and was frustrated those keys were not turning up. The more Anthea looked, the further away they seemed to be.

The curves of the key give the impression there would continually be more questions with more clues along the curves of life. Continuing curves that never end. The keys hung on a wall that unlock the case. Everyone needs keys to unlock knowledge. Katy for her journalism, Anthea for her past life, though not today they were still in hiding. Knowledge was what she wanted and yearned to catch up on, she lost it all by having had a sheltered childhood.

Her mother was sick, suffering from a mental illness, which prevented her from living life to the fullest. She suffered the shame, inferiority. Back when Anthea was in the little white socks, it was shameful to be mentally sick.

Longing for the information and truth of who she was and where she belonged, Anthea needed comfort in her brain, like a chess game; if you don't know the rules, the game will be lost. She had missed normal life and had much to share with the world. Many things to bring to the light. 'What is the truth everybody is searching for?'

thought Anthea. Truth regarding life, truth about death, truth regarding anything. Is truth in the eye of the beholder? One-man's truth is another man's lie?' and so her thoughts bounced.

No one could teach you; it was the quest for the wisdom, knowledge and understanding that must give the answers. One thing she knew, the words Papa once said to her at CaféB rang true. "When you receive some information, check its reliability before you act upon it." Anthea moved on to her day, leaving the book on the table. She was exhausted, but the world would be changed. Truth conveyed, transported to its rightful place. We all know; we just need to find it. The keys are in us; all we want is peace of mind.

The secret is in the Suitcase…

The Elephant in the room steals the truth and hides it. The Answer is hiding in the Ping-Pong Balls. Finding the puzzle pieces will be costly.

Anthea let out a sigh, smiled and covered over her frustration with the knowledge she was going to find all her answers.

In everyone, there is something precious found in no one else." [unknown]

Having a good role model was also important in life, no matter which part of history or race or gender that person was.

Eleanor Roosevelt once said, "The future belongs to those who believe in the beauty of their dreams." Knowledge Rules….

Thank you, Table 31.

You are the Keeper of the 'Knowledge' and the best part of my day.

The TRUTH has set me free to be all I can be in this life.

L

CHAPTER 12

Lavinia

Lavinia Little White Socks

Loneliness

Crinkled Auburn leaves were a beautiful sight. These natural colours of the season gave all the information that winter was closing in, boisterously nudging Autumn out of the way. Lavinia loved this time of year with its vibrant colours, smells, and sounds. She felt energised and happy with the changing of seasons.

Lavinia was from Latvia and had met Lucy on a train trip through Europe in their late teens. Coincidentally, their mothers were close friends and became neighbours in London. One of her mother's closest friends was a woman called Stella Joy. Lavinia remembered her mother's quarrels with Stella and how sad and upset she became through this friendship. Lavinia loved the red woollen cape that Stella wore, which smelled of a particular perfume that, if Lavinia caught a breath of it now, made her feel sick. One morning at CaféB, sitting across from Anthea and Lavinia was a silver-haired lady with a grey coat on. There was no colour about her, and she reminded Lavinia of her mother. Memories jump around like flies in a dark cave, glow worms that you can't catch hold of.

Many years ago in Latvia, her mother told the story of how Autumn was a sad time of year. It reminded her of feeling lonely, lying on the ground, being kicked out of the home, cold, sad, beautiful colours fading fast. Ambers, ochres, and reds- her colours faded fast many years ago. The silver hair, and grey coat were the data that triggered the memory for Lavinia.

The girls continued sharing memories from the data bank. Anthea remembered how a change in sock size was so exciting for her as she grew up through her childhood years. Little white socks on Anthea's growing feet were proof that adulthood was approaching and childhood was fast leaving her world. She dreamed of the time when she could do and express exactly what she wanted, omitting the word 'cannot' from her life and facing the world with full enthusiasm.

Little white socks soon turned into long white socks, then stockings. The seasons of life showed visual signs as much as the leaves falling from the mature trees. The leaves were beautiful, those fashionable colours suited her skin type. Lavinia loved the familiarity that facts gave her. Hugs were familiar facts. Anthea knew she was loved, and felt the security that brought, and with this knowledge, she was able to do battle with her internal demons.

Once an adult at eighteen, freedom was exhilarating. However, there were plenty of times she missed her little white socks. The security, comfort, and belonging that age brought her, that season of her life, now over. Some nights, even at eighteen, she would come home from the freedom of a party or weekend away, finding her emotions were not in the same space as her body. Many a morning her pillow was wet, and often she woke up tightly hugging it, as if it was going to be stolen from her. She missed the mother she yearned for, the one who never knew or understood her. Nevertheless, mother did make great bread pudding, and knit, and build a cosy fire. Anthea did not dwell there for too long. It cost her too much, and she was unable to pay the price for those emotions.

Lavinia Lucy Lily

Anthea believed colours had the power to heal from the inside out, and the outside in. Healing without leaving a complete carnage of emotions within the mind. When seeing someone who just pulls everything apart. She needed to discover that art of healing. First, though, she needed to connect deeper into the soul, and find her spiritual antenna. Like a radio, she knew it was imperative to tune into the right station based on knowledge, and truth. How was that going to be accomplished?

At that moment of peace, the café doors flung open. In came her whirlwind friends, Lavinia with Lucy, and Lily on each arm. What a surprise to see Lily. Lucy had on a sky-blue jacket, reminding Anthea of her outfit from her *trampoline* days. She had kept the special badge she won for her bronze medallion, followed by the silver a few years later. She was proud to remember being a coach, and a judge for international performances, it was a fantastic achievement. She remembered the excitement of the atmosphere and the smell of sweaty feet.

The three girls spent time in the club, practising twists, tucks, and pikes on Thursday nights. That sport lasted several years, until life took them on different paths. 'We were all so thin in those days, and wore clothes half the size of today's wardrobe,' thought Anthea.

CaféB Lavenders' Birthday

Poges had hung a beautiful bunch of pink, and mauve balloons from the ceiling as a surprise for Lavender, who was dreading her fortieth birthday.

Anthea had woken up feeling immensely joyful at the coming day, and was always pleased when time allowed the four or five if Lavender turns up, to have a day of laughter after the long-suffering she had confronted all week. Unbelievable, if it were not so frustrating, it would be laughable. Lost stock, a shattered window, wrong gender models, one of which had two left arms, and the stupidity of the window display company sending fake snow, and giant snowflakes instead of giant beach balls, sand, and deck chairs.

The waste of energy, time, and paperwork was too much to bear, along with numerous things she dared not begin to remember before work, knowing the big red clock never cared that she needed more time this morning, or every morning.

Anthea took the first sip of the heavenly coffee sitting seductively in her favourite mug before her as she cupped her hands around it, letting the warmth radiate through her chilled fingers. Typical English winter coming on, summer was not much better.

Lavinia Hit by Grief

Lavinia had just lost her job due to the closure of the hotel where she was a chambermaid. The owners had gone into insolvency due to tax fraud. The inspectors had been around to do a spot check on the hotel books, and had uncovered a lot of book keeping transgressions. The two owner managers, known as the *Bova Brothers*, were found to be lying about the number of guests per week, and the expenses did not add up with their exotic lifestyle. A typical business running two sets of books. It was their youngest disabled brother who had spilt the beans on the hotel.

The brothers had fallen out over money, and there was the small incident of the wife-swapping saga. Neighbours had been whispering about the goings on, and the youngest brother, Lionel, found the opportunity to spill his knowledge to the taxman. He was making his moral criticism recognised, anticipating that his elder brother's judgement day was looming. Lavinia never saw it coming, had not prepared ahead of time, living day to day, not seeing what was in front of her, living as if life were easy, and free. No storing grain in a barn for her, or preparing for drought. No rainy days. Her drought had now hit her. Feeling devastated, she needed a time-out with friends.

Anthea had been noticing her withdrawal of late. Lavinia's sorrow at losing her job, was accentuated by the fact that Lucy had finally been given a large part in a new television series, and was happy her career received an excellent kick start after many years of frustrating bit parts, getting small solitary pieces with hardly enough money to pay rent, and food. Some days she had to choose. Now, she could afford both, and holidays too.

This was thrilling for Lucy. They celebrated, laughed, and enjoyed the time. Still waiting for the arrival of Lavender, who had been somewhat scared to turn forty, and had not yet conceived her first child, she was determined to make it a great decade after a rather nasty breakdown following a divorce. It had been far more painful than she could have imagined. Big subjects.

Windows at Lake Windermere

Anthea, now aged ninety-nine, cosy and in her wooden cottage, gazed out from her writing room window. The Raven gazed back at her in a knowing way, with his head tilted. Anthea wondered if ravens have memories, 'of course they do,' she thought. This raven had seen so much of her life, and still knew where to find the pine tree. Her thoughts appeared to her as if it were yesterday, as if no time had passed. Her focus shifted to a gust of wind which came from nowhere, her eyes just caught a glimpse of that cloak, disappearing into the pine trees. She took a deep breath, wondering if she would ever finish her book. Tell about the woman in the red cloak, talk about what happened to the café, and would Anthea finish the story about the suitcase, and the truth it was hiding?

Her shaking hand poised the pen to paper, and swiftly continued with her biography. Elegantly, her writing kept on growing as she put together the experiences of the wonderful days of her youth, parties, and laughter, remembering all the fun, sadness, shared stories, and indiscretions that filled her life so long ago. Many friends came, and went, died, or moved, yet were still able to remain present in her world through her memories. She stopped writing for a few seconds, and paused before adding her next chapter on life at CaféB. Yes, shortly after Lavinia had lost her job, Lucy scored a movie part, and Lavender just turned forty. I, the writer, Anthea, was dealing with wrong gender manikins, and a boisterous suitcase. Life.

Lavinia's loneliness was unremitting, her feelings of uselessness grew more apparent. Why did she feel lonely when her friends all surrounded her, loved her? Feeling isolated, in amongst well-connected friendships seemed absurd, though no one wholly understood Lavinia or was able to connect deeply to her soul. Something that takes time, skill, energy, and is costly, and opens the big doors of vulnerability. Though the subjects were heavy, the fun atmosphere was growing.

Papa had been writing his journal, or was it a book? He was a small part of the café life, but a big part of Anthea's life. He was recording the thoughts, motives, and intents of each character. This was going to be one hefty book. Never a day passed that he did not sit at the same table, or have fish, and wine for lunch. He was healthy, never had a sick day in his life. Heard everything and missed nothing.

Café Day at the Races

Poges had been particularly jolly that morning as he had become the proud owner of a part share in a racehorse. Her stable name was 'Lightning.' Great name for a racehorse, he joked, as he bounced around the café all morning. A better name than 'Loose Lady' or 'Jenny come lately,' he joked. "Chipper," Anthea said as the three girls waltzed up towards the bar to make their orders.

Poges nearly choked on his lime drink at their flamboyancy, and cheek. Anthea ordered iced liquorice tea for Lucy, a Lime Lemon Martini for herself, and Lily. Lavinia had the long black with hot milk on the side, always was quite specific about this. "People are very particular about what they drink, no sugar large mug, not a cup, some would choose their mug colour, and that could change everyday" said Poges.

Lavinia was a little irritated by the energy Poges had, and made a rude comment regarding his age, and how he should grow up, act his age. He laughed a long loud Irish laugh replying "don't you worry girls, when there's snow on the mountain, and the trees are bare, there's still plenty of heat in the valley." Lavinia was not amused, was irritated about many things, and was still suffering from terrible homesickness after having moved from her home in Tasmania to take up residence in Britain due to her husband's work.

Lavinia had never felt so lonely. While she was reluctant to reveal feelings, or open totally, her sadness stemmed from the fact she had no family near her. Mother, father, sisters, brothers, cousins, aunts, uncles, as if an avalanche or a tidal wave had wiped them out. Or a house fire. Family gone. It felt worse that they were still alive, but she was unable to see them.

Lavinia had no finances to go back, and forth for a visit to her overseas family. She had missed two weddings, a funeral, two baptisms, and had not seen three nieces since they were born. Anthea failed to understand how she could have done it, to pack up, and leave with a few small cartons, it was all the belongings she had been allowed to take by husband. He controlled every detail in her life. Lavinia's friends or family rarely acknowledged her unhappiness or traumas. Despite all that they were great friends. Anthea was thankful. Yes, all supported one another through thick, and thin times.

However, because Lavinia hid her unhappiness, no one knew anything. Friends stick together through the nitty-grittiest of life. Hard times, bad times, great times. A supportive family, was the one thing she truely wanted but it was stripped from her with a massive move overseas some five years earlier. Lavinia had no say in the decision to move away. It was all controlled by the man she was set to marry, and subsequently did marry. This family were all controlled by the father. It was rarely discussed with Lavinia who was simply expected to go along with the family plans. She was both immature, naïve, and utterly traumatized. She had imagined a good future ahead, swept in the romance of it all.

Poges asked where the birthday girl was, remembering it was Lavender's birthday today, she ought to have already arrived. Everything was perfect except for the missing Lavender. They had organised an "L" day for the birthday. A tradition that had started many years ago. So unusual to get the entire group with names that begin with "L" for London, or "L" for Lamington, "L for anything" squealed Lucy. Lavinia, Lily, Lucy, and Anthea did not pay much attention to the clock that morning.

Anthea wore her Lilac dress, she loved it. Having put a small flashing Christmas tree on her lapel leftover from the last Christmas in July café brunch, she really felt in the season to be jolly. Poges had put a beautiful, gaudy Christmas bunting, and an electronic lotus lily, with flashing lights on the table.

It was a silken square box, lined with some electronic wires, typically him. He was not a person to spend money on Christmas decorations because people would steal them. He did however enjoy the fun side. "Ghastly" remarked Lily, laughing at Poges trying to hide the fact it was fake silk, and electronic, by putting it in a box with water in it to make it look realistic, and fresh. Anthea was amazed by his creativity, loved how each day he changed the table decoration for her, allowing the thought that she was special.

Lotus lily floating in soft red water for Christmas. She adored his creativity, and sentiment. That was good data. Anthea liked the green, and red card that lit up with sparkles equally as tasteless as the plastic-lined box. She enjoyed his sense of fun, and freedom to over exaggerate the tacky tinsel, glitter, and baubles, it added a personal touch for all the people who read this card during the day ahead. It was a line taken from a poem by a favourite poet Emerson. Ralf Waldo Emerson. It read:

The Earth Laughs in Flowers.

"I love that," said Anthea. Crying was how the heart speaks, yet lips could not explain the pain. 'Did her heart feel different from her mind?' She caught herself sliding into more profound thought.

Lavender Birthday Girl

It was not the morning for this type of pondering. Her thoughts rang in her ears like tinnitus on a windy day, times a hundred, having already experienced tinnitus once or twice after being walloped around the ears, 'do not go there,' she ordered her mind, her pinging thoughts, 'do not complain' said the sharp voice inside her head. Anthea looked up quite shocked, almost as if the table had spoken to her. In front of Anthea stood the birthday girl Lavender, relieved for the distraction of her colourful, loud arrival. Anthea chuckled at Lavender's adornment in her hair, and wondered if she had been drinking again. Maybe a wine or two. She had a Christmas hat on covered in fake lavender sprigs, silk ones from the local shop. They all laughed as she told the girls, and anyone else who would listen, she could not find any mistletoe, all sold out.

Lavender had to do the next best thing using lavender sprigs, they continued with their laughter. She looked great saying "Do not complain." She laughed out loud dancing around singing "kiss me under the mistletoe." "Complain? Why would I do that"? Anthea chuckled, and twirled the happy birthday girl, Lavender Jayne, amongst the hilarious laughter. "I have no complaints; you are extremely artistic to swap mistletoe for lavender" squealed Anthea amongst the continuing laughter.

Anthea noticed Mr Grey had not arrived that morning which meant it was more relaxed in the places where 'relaxed' could reside in parts of her mind. She also noticed in the garden by the tree, Poges had changed the sign. He must have found another Irish proverb. It read thus: *When you have only two pennies left in the world buy a loaf of bread with one, and a lily with the other.*

'Interesting' thought Anthea just as a baker's van trundled past the café, pulled by a Shire-horse. A traditional scene at Christmas along the busy streets of London. Oxford Street was filled with decorations, an abundance of fabulous beautiful brightly coloured ribbons symbolising the Holy season around Europe, and the world.

The girls danced in the street, danced in the café, and totally immersed themselves in the party atmosphere of all things tinsel, and Christmas. Singing joy to the world, and hark the herald, blending in with I'm dreaming of a white Christmas, they knew the medley's off by heart. Not one Santa song to be heard, no Rudolph, and no jingle bells made it all the more delightful. They did however enjoy a few rounds of Slades *Merry Christmas Song* which reminded Anthea of her cousins, and delightful times with Brian at *Harali* every Christmas. It was the most popular 'pub song' of the seventies. The girls sang at the tops of every octave possible.

Trip to Cornwall

Anthea was extremely satisfied with her current job as a window dressing artiste. Busy, vibrant, a fabulous job especially at this time of year. Having recently returned from her an enlightening train trip to Cornwall, paid for by an award she won for the bestdressed window that month, and was the worthy recipient of the *Around United Kingdom* British rail prize, and chose to spend the 500 pounds seeing all of Cornwall, where they all speak with a fascinating accent, sounding like farmers.

Her trip began at a hotel in Lizard Point, well known for the cliffs, geology, and coastal scenery, the south western most point is the famous Land's End, and the southernmost part of Lizard Point. Two hundred, and sixteen miles from London, it's a fabulous train trip. Cornish history, and civilization dates back to the Palaeolithic Age which is characterized by the use of chiselled or 'knapped' stone tools. Definitely old stone age, and one of Anthea's interests.

Anthea came back to London with a few Cornish words, and tried to use them sometime during the day at work. 'Allycumpooster' meaning all in order, everything is all right, one she used frequently. Without practice, the words would slip into the compartment of lost things, lost words being the main category. Closely guarded by the grey ball marked *'Useless,'* and his friend *'Mislaid'*.

Once in that compartment of the little brown suitcase, they rarely came out. Sometimes they were let out on bail, but almost always returned. Bail was paid for by the smart ball called *Charity*, a lovely cherry red colour. *A Crib* is a midmorning snack, not going for a snooze she laughed when telling Poges of her new words. *Cack* is another word for excrement, often used as a swear word, well it did for sure impress all her friends, and confuse the bosses at work. Poges used it behind the bar whenever he dropped a glass.

She had met a very friendly woman from Penzance whilst on the train, where the weather is often 'Dummity,' overcast or dreary. They stayed friends for many years after her trip had ended, and met up once a year somewhere new for Anthea in Cornwall.

One of her favourite stories she heard were of the 'Knockers' which are the spirits that dwell underground, and haunt the villages each night. Anthea loved all the old tales, and shared them with terrified *Tacker's*, or small children for fun. Poges had nieces, and nephews who loved to hear stories about the famous *Penzance Pirates. Cornwall stirs your wanderlust* she agreed with the saying on a postcard she kept on her cork board. After Penzance, she spent a few days exploring the tiny village called Mousehole, so called for the one small cave resembling a 'mouse hole.' This was where Anthea stayed at the famous *Lobster Pot* guest house. The famous writer *Dylan Thomas* who wrote the Welsh play Undermilk Wood, and where his new wife Caitlin McNamara spent their honeymoon after marrying in Penzance. Anthea was there in time for the local festival, which was the inspiration behind the book called *The Mousehole Cat' by Antonia Barber*. This festival is also the origin of 'Star Gazey Pie', a mixed fish, egg, and potato pie with fish heads protruding through the pastry. 'Quite hideous, and too scary to eat' grimaced Anthea. After Mousehole, next stop was an ancient castle.

Saint Michaels Mount

A fascinating castle on an island, across the water. It was here Anthea discovered her new Cornish word Quignogs or ridiculous notions. The castle was a highlight for Anthea who loved the old coats of Armour, cannons, and medieval battle rooms. The helmet for protection of the brain, the mind, the thoughts, and beliefs, all contained inside the head. If the helmet was insecure, you would die for sure.

Anthea wondered what those walls had seen…oh how she would love to have a means of visiting that part of history, but only for an hour, to see the hustle, and bustle of the servant's quarters. She stooped through ancient doorways, and imagined the goings on of 17th century life between those cold walls set high upon cold rocks, in a cold sea. History & legends were plentiful, endless tales, and accounts that rise on the tide as if they came from the deep caves under the sea. Her imagination ran wild hearing about such stories as *Cormoran the Giant*, civil war soldiers, and fishermen. She could hear the sounds, the voices emanating from the cracks in the walls, as if they were alive today, or at least their spirits were, hearing pilgrim's bare feet padding across the causeway, soldier's heavy leather boots racing up to the battlements during the *Wars of the Roses*. The chant of monks praying in the priory, the smell of canon gunpowder in the air, the thud of butter churning in the dairy.

The island was also an important landmark for spiritual seekers who explored its unique energy thanks to age-old ley lines which course under the sea, and crossed at the heart of the Mount. Gossip, and whispers were something Anthea had suffered in the office, gossip amongst friends, and family, all stemming from judgement. Whispers, stories, and judgements all brought with them a sentence of death in those days, and in today's world, it is a death of a different kind yet equally as painful.

The Cornish legend of *Jack the Giant Killer*, a gruesome beast who terrorised the land, stealing cattle when his tummy began to rumble. Anthea made the venture up the mount to find the giant's stone heart. Peering through the turrets, she watched boats bobbing on to the harbour, where ships once creaked, loaded with Cornish tin, and where traders made their fortunes. Her imagination was in overdrive. By the time of the Norman conquest in 1066, Saint Michael's Mount had come into the possession of the monks of its sister isle, Mont-Sant-Michel in Normandy France. Anthea had popped across the channel to France, and visited the identical sister castle. Such a fascinating part of her trip.

Site of Conflict

Anthea gazed out across the rows of cannons which once drove a Napoleonic ship to its capture on Marazion beach. She stood at the top of the church tower where the first beacon was lit that warned London of the approach of the Spanish Armada. Conflict. That was a subject that ripped friends apart, broke families, and slashed career prospects. Conflicts of personality, of belief systems, of political viewpoints, stuff that all wars are made of. Power, and control go hand in hand with gossips, and hearsay. Twins, like the two castles.

Her second last town to visit was Lands-End. Anthea's funniest word learnt from her trip to Cornwall was *Fizzogg* or face, and is used quite commonly around the towns, pubs, and in social situations. Lands-End, a headland in western Cornwall, eight miles or thirteen kilometres west-south-west of Penzance. To the east of it is the English Channel, and to the west the Celtic Sea. Anthea always loved to know where she was, and which ocean was closest to her feet. She fell in love with Cornwall as a child, and it never left her soul.

St. Ives

Her last day was spent at Saint Ives, the place reminded her of an old nursery rhyme, "I met a man at Saint Ives, he had so many wives" she could not sing the rest, humming along to the tune as she walked through the town. It became one of those thoughts, that once stuck in your head, repeats itself over, and over, like a song that you'd rather not keep singing. Fudge, and ice-cream, was her next stop. A quaint café on the edge of the street, on the pavement, a few inches from the edge of the road. 'These streets are ridiculously narrow' she laughed to herself. Here she learnt the word *Zackley* as she paid for her afternoon tea, meaning exactly. Her money was correct.

She met a new friend called Jan who worked at the castle giving tours, what a brilliant mind she had, remembering all that history, a beautiful lady who remained friends with Anthea up until the future took them both away in different directions.

'Sadly, it seems impossible to stay friends with every lovely person you meet on holiday's thought Anthea, 'maybe someone will someday invent a method of staying in touch with everybody you ever meet, whether you like them or not, there will be no lost connections' that was a funny thought. Anthea often had inventions she made up in her mind, 'solutions to problems' she called them.

Saint Ives was named from an Irish princess, and missionary called Saint Ia. According to the story Jan told Anthea, Saint Ia sailed from Ireland to Cornwall on a leaf, way back in the 5th Century. Stennack means *place of tin*. Anthea, and Jan were booked onto the tin mine tour, such a fascinating afternoon. Anthea hardly wanted to leave.

Oh, how she treasured Cornwall. However, she was yet to find out why her connections seemed so strong, after all they were only childhood holidays she was retracing, maybe there was more to Cornwall to come, would she end up there again one day? Cobbled Cornwall with funny, strange accents. The west country. Her head was filled with delightful memories from childhood when she wore those little white socks, and held her mother's hands.

Brown Shoes. Lace-Ups

Slade Christmas music was still playing, and Anthea had enjoyed a beautiful Christmas carol service at the old castle in Cornwall, where she could have sworn, she saw Papa. The man was so real, she tapped him on the shoulder, but he walked through the *Armoury*, and never saw him again on that trip.

Today however, Papa the ancient gentleman as Anthea called him, who occupied the same seat every day at CaféB, wore a brown rain mac. It was threatening to rain, preparation was his forte, a tweed jacket did not quite fit the bill that day. Though continually well-groomed, he sometimes wore a creamy beige jumper with a lime green tie. He seemed to be constantly writing doing crosswords or making written entries in a notebook. She asked him about Cornwall, but he simply smiled, and said "I'll write about it." 'What a strange man he is' she thought. 'Does anyone understand him?' she wondered, other than he loves green.

He had made a fulfilling friend of Poges who also loved green, mainly green tight pants. Anthea was at a friend's wedding many years earlier with Poges, he wore his tight green pants. 'Was Papa Irish' she wondered? He did seem to relate to every nationality which she found strange as normally people relate only to their own. Those memories made her smile, along with the sounds outside the café.

The Christmas bells were calling out the myriads of Christmas songs over the speakers. Light, love, liberty, and life were freely in high supply. Papa had a favourite quote, and would often tell Anthea "The secret things belong to the Lord, and not to us" though we hoped they did. Secrets were revealed in the fullness of time, rarely ever at a human speed, she heard that from somewhere once. 'Perhaps it was from Papa,' she thought. He seemed to know a lot of secret things, he said "seek them, find them, find the knowledge hidden in them." Anthea really liked Papa; he intrigued her. 'Did he write them or just read them?' she wondered. Those heavy books in a robust grey case.

Lavinia Hides Her Pain

Lucy, and Lily begged Anthea to tell one of her stories before work called an end to the frivolities. The story of her train trip. She obliged. Lily, Lavender complimented with energetic clapping as Anthea took a little bow, and began. "I was half an hour away from pulling in after a long journey through the Cornish grey quaintly assembled towns to the last stop Penzance." Anthea continued. "I had a good sleep despite the bumpy, shaky bed I was in. Shaking my body up like a milkshake as the train whirled around many corners.

Unexpectedly, abruptly, the whole train came to a sudden halt. All was quiet. For a few minutes I awoke, still half-dreaming, it was as if I was on the Orient Express, I loved it." Anthea continued. "I was in the movie, there were noises throughout the train, screaming, grinding like breaking metal. Noises sounded terrible, ear-splitting. Awful screaming, deep scary screaming" she animated the horror with exaggeration leaving the girl's faces looking shocked at the table. Lavinia turned white, feeling unable to contribute to the fun. Lucy's eyes popped wider than her sockets. "A murder" said Anthea eyes wide open, loud enough for the café to start staring. The frivolity continued. Anthea also continued. "I jumped up out of my narrow bed still thinking I was in a double bed at Jan's house, my new Cornish friend where I was the day before the train trip. The train rocked, and I fell, crashed into the large metal door as the train tilted, I flew out into the hallway of the train carriage, floor space the size of a pantry realising my lace lemon nightie had dropped to my knees." Chaos erupted. "Check the murder horror of all horrors," squealed Lucy. Anthea continued, "a lady had fallen off her top bunk, a rather sudden end to her sleep, breakfast was twenty minutes late. I was starving," recalled Anthea. "I was not complaining, just still waking up. This was all true, she shrieked."

The girls looked suspicious. "I was happily almost in Plymouth, not on the *Murder on the Orient Express* as I had thought, though I did have a lovely shower in the minuscule ensuite on the train. Swinging like a monkey from side to side as the train sped up to make up for lost time that was caused by some thugs who had stolen some copper wiring from the signal boxes along the line. The girls were still shrieking with laughter after the copper wiring incident, they wanted this story to go on all morning. "I felt like a squash ball, flung from wall to wall." She animated with her hands, showing toothbrush indentations in her cheeks. That was her workout for the morning.

Lavinia Loneliness

Anthea finished her recollections of this part of the trip. The girls all roared with hilarity, Lavender sprayed the floor with her birthday cake as she could scarcely contain her laughter. Anthea noticed Lavinia was a little quieter than usual this morning.

'Maybe she had a bug, or a worry' thought Anthea. The girls continued the birthday brunch. Time was ticking, it was getting late in the morning. Lucy left, followed by Lily, and Lavender. Lavinia said her goodbyes, with extra-long hugs before rushing into the ladies WC. They all embraced, and departed, Anthea thanking Poges enormously. He adored her, she loved him. Sadly, they might never be destined for each other as life did not travel down the same road, and stole the two of them apart. A fun-filled morning with her closest of friends shortly came to an end.

The WC door opened, outraced a lady in a red woollen cape, in a hurry, she screamed, screamed mightily for help, 'perhaps she had dropped her mobile phone down the toilet' thought Anthea, 'that would be enough to make anyone cry.' She frowned a disapproving frown, 'what a carry-on, thinking she had too much wine at lunch.'

Anthea tried to console the distressed red caped woman who dragged Anthea into the WC, the lady's bathroom. 'Goodness' thought Anthea as she rushed towards the door, halting abruptly, like the train with no copper wiring. Her mouth dropped open, her throat closed over as her eyes scanned the small room, she saw her beloved friend Lavinia on the floor, slumped up against the toilet door. Bleeding, red, still warm blood. Red as the Christmas lights in Oxford Street. Blood everywhere, she stared, unable to process or believe this was Lavinia. Anthea could not move. She fell to the floor; her muscles gave way unable to move into the next moment. Believing her mind was heartlessly, cruelly tricking her as she heard the sirens coming closer.

Poges cleared the onlookers away as Anthea's head fell to the floor. She hugged her friend, screamed a hard, harrowing scream knowing it would not wake her. Wrists, legs slit wide open, blood gushing, knife on the floor close to her hand. Time stood still seeming like a hundred years.

Anthea, gently led away by the ambulance man who got as far as the table, and stopped. 'It did not feel like it was her' she thought, feeling like an onlooker, and that this moment did not belong to her. Anthea screamed, hung onto the table cloth of happiness, laughter draped the beautiful happy birthday that only moments earlier had the four girls creating Merry Christmas mayhem together around the cake.

Her body seemed to float up to watch the scene from above a streetlamp, then coming back to earth again as she felt strong kind arms around her. Anthea pulled the cloth, clutching at the white linen, the lotus flower dropped to the floor. She felt the fear rise, burning in her mouth, shaking from the centre of her bones.

The kind-hearted empathetic grace-filled ambulance man wrapped Anthea in the white linen, as he did, a note dropped from the cloth to the floor. Leck, according to his badge, the ambo man, picked it up, held it in his hand. His blood ran cold as he read it. He saw the red splats, splashes of blood on Anthea, which once held life in Lavinia, now mingled on the linen cloth with cake, and sandwiches crumbs. The candles dropped to the lotus lilies. Leck gave the note to Poges whose café was now a crime scene. Police, ambulance, fire brigade swarming. Had the lady in red become a suspect, the one who came out from the toilet screaming, no one knew anything at this point?

The shock set in rapidly. Lavinia's body, taken out on a stretcher covered with a white linen cloth. Anthea screamed the deepest of howling yelps like an animal caught in a trap, a trap of despair, horror, and disbelief, as she tried to remain with her friend. The two were taken towards the waiting ambulances. Lavinia's lifeless, limp body wheeled away. Poges, and Anthea hugged, held one another, hands shaking they read the note.

It read:

"Loneliness was not my friend.
The lighthouse on the horizon
shines its light. However,
the rocks were hard. Too dark.
The flower withers, yet the seed remains.
There is no death. Be careful who you trust.
The Devil was once an Angel.
I must go. I love you, dearly yet cannot stay.
Forgive me,
Lavinia the new seed."

The subject of loneliness was never mentioned, nor encouraged. To speak about it was not easy. It involved a lifetime of unhealthy patterns, so as if it were a failure, Lavinia chose to keep it tucked away. It was incurable even though she had good friends, she just hid her pain, fear of being mis-understood, imprisoned her true self.

Elephants Room

Anthea's body shuddered as if it were zero degrees as a female police officer emerged holding a plastic bag with the red as a robin knife in it. Swiftly it was taken away. The knife held life, death in its power. Anthea had no idea Lavinia was suicidal. If only she had known. Did any of them know? The subject of death was never mentioned between them yet were a close, unified, girlfriend group. Anthea, telling the police everything she knew, realised it was not enough.

Where was the truth of Lavinia's heart that bled dry, spilt her own life on the cold white marble floor? How could she be lonely? We were a group, we were all friends, family, secure, tight, caring, how could loneliness scourge its way in? The realisation Anthea, and the others did not know until the too late sign had commenced flashing before her in neon lights.

Shock hit her hard, the complete realisation the truth had remained covered, never exposed. How would she ever get through the sorrow, the guilt? The laughter had turned merciless. The table would never recover from this. Life could never improve. Friendship. Deep yet shallow, how could that be? Pathways, never straight, always curved, crooked. Anthea's thoughts just rambled, tumbling around her head like a clothes dryer, trying to iron out the creases in precious fabric.

Thoughts all jumbled, unrecognisable as logic they disappeared into the table. Anthea could not grasp what had just happened. How could sleep ever bring peace? That note. The cruel letter was all she had left. Unrecoverable. Too tragic, too many unanswered questions, ones where there were no answers. Sadness steals happiness, the rock, paper, scissors game, however, this was no game. The reality would take Anthea days, weeks to begin to set in. Maybe months, years, if ever. Death seemed to have the last laugh. Where was the lighthouse now?

Lavinia lost her breath, her blood, her strength. Minutes had become hours at table31, where memories leak, and the tales told. Where coffees calmed nerves, soothe spirits. No amount of coffee could help her now. The prettiest smile hid the most profound secrets. The sweetest eyes cried the deepest tears. The kindest hearts have held the most pain. Where now was kindness.

Poges was ushered outside along with the entire café of happiness. Joy had gone; the restaurant closed until further notice. This death, Anthea hung her head. She glanced at a patch of red berries on the ground from the tree Poges had decorated, stared at them as the realisation Lavinia's pain was hidden from them all. This, the last supper, the last time together. What do you do with awareness once you realise? How do you cope? This question left her as cold as the blood left behind. All the pain fell on the unsympathetic hard slate of the toilet floor. The red berries turned grey as the undigested birthday cake in Anthea's vomit hit the hard ground. Stillness cloaked the scene.

The Lesser Spotted Woodpecker somewhere in the world warbled a happy song.

"Do not squander time, for that is the stuff life is made of"

[Benjamin Franklin]

Table 31, recovery from loneliness is your priority.

Sometimes the head needs more time to accept what your heart already knows. You are valuable.

www.ingramcontent.com/pod-product-compliance
Lightning Source LLC
Chambersburg PA
CBHW071427300726

48976CB00004B/1260